THE CURSE OF TIME

The Curse of Time

ANDREEA PRYDE

Independently Published

Chapter 1

I never believed in the paranormal. Curses, enchantments, lucky amulets, evil spirits, angels, demons, heaven, and hell–all this meant nothing more than fantasies found between the covers of a book. Fantasies meant to influence weak minds, yet, despite all that, I got the job.

How *and* Why?

I said all these things, and quite clearly, I might add, in front of the Director. The result? I was utterly ignored, but then again, why did I take on the offer? Maybe because on the paper, the salary, the bonuses, and the benefits looked extremely appealing. I'm not superficial, but I like to live comfortably, and my university degree doesn't give me too many opportunities. If I'm aiming for a career in this field, I can't afford to be picky. I must take everything that comes my way, no matter what.

I was officially employed at the **Occultism, Witchcraft, and Magical Artefacts History Museum**. What a fancy name for a place full of lies and charades.

I let my head fall on the desk loaded with piles of books, manuscripts, parchments, and some of the strangest objects I've ever seen, which had to be restored, classified, and only then, prepared for display.

There was only one big problem; I knew nothing about the objects in front of me, of which I was, anyway, convinced to the marrow of my bones that they were nothing more than rubbish meant to take money from poor suckers who believed.

I needed coffee, loads, and loads of coffee.

I returned from the small staff kitchenette with a steaming cup of coffee in my hand, only to bump my nose into the freshly mounted sign on my office/workshop door.

SCARLETT AUBYN
RESTAURATOR AND CLASSIFIER
OF ARTEFACTS AND OCCULT DOCUMENTS

I wanted to rip the sign–together with the door it was glued on–into pieces, and it was only the second week of work. I wondered what the next phase was. Fight with the exhibits? Scream at the visitors? Sleep in a coffin? Or maybe the worst possibility of them all–to believe all this was real.

A soft knock on the door interrupted my descent into the dark abyss of the shadows of despair, and inside the room, stepped a woman. Laura had worked as a guide for this place for over twenty years, and also, she was the only one who welcomed me with a big, warm smile.

In the two weeks since I started working here, I haven't seen any of the museum employees, except for the day the Director introduced me to the team. A small team formed out of four people, apart from him.

The first one was Matteo, the secretary; an introverted young man, with dark hair and pale skin, rocking a nerdy look, but without much of a presence, who greeted me almost inaudibly without moving his gaze from the floor. By his side stood Gregor, the housekeeper; a grumpy, old Russian man, who'd worked in the museum for almost all his life and from who I couldn't hear more than a low grunt. Next in line was Silvia from the gift-shop. The young woman was too busy playing with her blonde hair, making loud-bursting bubbles out of chewing gum, and looking at her long, fake nails to pay me any sort of attention. And last, but not least, the woman who stood now in front of me, Laura.

"Am I bothering you?" she asked politely.

"No, not at all! To be fair, I was just starting to feel a bit lonely," I said, getting on my feet as she got closer.

"Well then, that means I got here just in time. Tell me, did you manage to get used to this place yet?" She smiled in a friendly way.

"Not quite. I find it a bit difficult, to be honest, mostly because I have no idea where to begin," I said, pointing at the piles on the desk and around it. "I managed to prepare a few parchments and books for display, but I'm currently facing a bit of a problem."

"Such as?" she pried. "You know, I've been working here for quite a while, so I might be able to help you here and there until you find your own way."

"For example, I have no idea what that is," I pointed my finger at a long wooden carving.

"That's a phallus," Laura said relaxed.

"A what?" I asked, thinking I must've heard wrong.

"A phallus," Laura repeated unbothered by my reaction.

"Okay, then what about this?" I showed her a very similar object, but this time out of metal.

"Also, a phallus. Anything else?" she asked joyfully.

"Alright, though I'm a bit scared to ask. What about this drawing?" I handed her one of the books lying around open. "The writing is quite washed away, so I can't decipher it all."

"Oh, now this is rather interesting," she said, fascinated. "This is a double-headed phallus used in harvest rituals."

"Double-headed!" my mouth fell open.

"Yup, there are with up to eight heads, but what goes over three were used for black magic."

"But why couldn't they use something else? I think I saw at least twenty similar objects and over a hundred drawings in the past several days."

"The obsession for power, I suppose. The man was considered the absolute power, after gods, at that time, and since the major belief was that his power came from his genitals, they used it for various rituals," she explained calmly.

"Wait. When you say 'used,' you mean . . .?"

"The organ," she continued my sentence.

"'The organ'?" I repeated shocked.

"If you ask me, this is exactly the reason why the Great Witch Hunt began, because the witches hunted men as well. The bigger and stronger the man, the more extraordinary the result, but when they began to no longer be able to acquire the needed materials, they became creative and improvised. And that's how these little guys came into existence. Depending on the ritual they were needed for, the witches crafted them from various materials. For example–for harvests, used wood, for strength, used metal, for wealth, gold and silver; for fertility, animal skin. As for those who had enough courage to practice black magic, they used them from corpses, which is why a phallus with more than three heads is an extremely rare sight."

I was as sickened as I could be and didn't want to listen to another word, but I had to ask; there was no way for me to keep my job if I didn't learn more.

"How do you know all that?"

"Oh, you poor thing, no one told you now, have they? We have a rather comprehensive library here with diverse witchcraft history books and case studies. Follow me, I'll show you."

"Lead the way."

I walked one step behind Laura, who opened the way towards a building's wing closed to the public. Somehow, I had the feeling I shouldn't be there at all, but I needed the money this job had to offer even if the place gave me chills and raised the hair on the back of my neck. Still following Laura, I thought the Gothic style she adopted didn't match her personality at all. The clothes, hair, nails, the heavy make-up, everything was black with a very white skin as a canvas. And her personality? Full of life, with a contagious smile, friendly and a little bit strange. Looking at her now, how she walked among the hall's shadows, like floating, she looked more like a witch or a vampire, than one of the museum's employees. She needed nothing more than a broom or a pair of fangs.

She stopped in front of a tall, white double door, and pushing them hard, she opened them, creating a loud squeak that spread throughout the building.

"I'm certain I've told Gregor countless times to oil these blasted doors," Laura snorted, moving inside the room, "but he keeps finding excuses not to come here. He says the place is cursed." She rolled her eyes.

"Cursed?" I asked, trying to hide the irony in my voice.

"Naive, right?" she laughed. "I mean all the cursed objects are displayed on the other side of the museum. Senile old man, he already forgot what madness is there on every single Halloween. It's like the whole museum would've moved in that room. Everyone comes for the Curses Exhibit and ignores the rest of the place whatsoever. Oh, well, either way, I don't think any of the curses are still active, after all, they won't last forever."

"Curses have an expiry date?" I asked a bit amused.

"Of course. They disappear in two situations; either the cursed one dies, or the one who threw the curse dies."

"So, no matter what, someone has to die?"

"Pretty much, but there is always the exception to the rule. There are powerful curses that never disappear, being directly linked to one's soul. Those connected to the body, disappear with it, but the soul is immortal."

I refrained from rolling my eyes, but instead, I tried to focus on the reason why I was in that room; research. Indeed, Laura said the library was ample, but I didn't take it too seriously. I was expecting maybe something between fifty and one hundred books, but there were at least a few hundreds. Books, files, studies, and journals, all arranged on different-looking shelves, or in boxes on the floor, gathering dust, touched only once in a long time.

"I know this might sound silly, but why are all the shelves so different from one another?" I asked, curious.

"That's easy. It's like a tradition."

"A tradition?" I asked, puzzled.

"The Director only buys a new shelf when there are enough books to fill it up, which sometimes can take several years. Look, there in the corner, the pièce de résistance."

I followed her with my eyes until she got near a huge shelf from the end of the 16th century. It wasn't difficult for me to recognise the shapes and decoration style; the complicated and elaborate combination of leaves, flowers, and angels. What I couldn't understand was what was such a carpentry master-piece doing in such a place covered by tons of dust?

"This should be in a museum, especially since it's in perfect shape!" I exclaimed.

"I remember suggesting something very similar to the Director at some point, but he said it's not possible. This shelf is the last thing left from his family's original fortune, and that he has no parting intentions."

Just then, a soft sound, like a cry, passed by my ear.

"Did you hear that?" I turned around.

Listening more closely, I walked in the direction in which I thought the sound came from, but I ended up facing with a wall, or at least, so I thought. At a closer look, I noticed concealed under the same shrivelled wallpaper as the rest of the room was a door, once secret.

"Hear what?" Laura asked me, curious.

"I thought I heard someone cry. I think it came from behind the door."

"That's impossible. In the next room, are nothing but the building's electric panels. You are standing in front of the plant room right there. Trust me when I tell you that no one goes in there for long periods of time. Maybe what you heard came from outside, but I heard nothing."

"Maybe . . ."

Maybe I heard things, perhaps it was all in my head, but why had I felt like I needed to get on the other side of the wall? Like something or someone was calling me. After all, there was nothing more than wires. Mentally, I slapped myself twice, and shaking off the unpleasant feeling, I returned to what was really important. I quickly picked a few titles that didn't seem like bedtime stories, and together with Laura, headed back. I highly doubt I could've found my way back all by myself.

"You know; I was sixteen years old when I started working here. My first part-time job," Laura started telling me, smiling. "I was such a hopeless romantic. I used to imagine that the grand exhibit hall was a ballroom where you could find the cream of society. Sometimes, when I was sure no one could see me, I was pretending to be a guest to such a ball," she said giggling.

"Well, considering the architectural style, I would say you're right. If my memory doesn't deceive me, and I doubt it because it was my favourite period, artistically speaking, this place was built at some point during the 16th century, so your imagination wasn't too far from reality. I can even imagine the music echoing throughout the building, colourful dresses swirling on the dancefloor, lovers flirting, young lads stealing a kiss or two under the moon from their partners. Even the room we just left from, perhaps at some point it was a study, or maybe a games room. If I could, I would renovate my house in this style; large windows, extravagant decorations, antique furniture," I said, dreaming with my eyes open.

"And here I thought I was the romantic one." Laura chuckled.

"I don't think it has anything to do with romanticism, but more with personal taste. All this had a certain elegance which can't be compared with anything from modern day, and probably, it never will have a comparison term ever again."

The way back seemed twice as long, the thick volumes making my arms go numb. Maybe I took one or two too many.

Once back, I thanked Laura for her help, and she waved me goodbye, closing the door behind her. I had less than half an hour until the end of my shift, so there was no point in engaging myself in something complicated. I looked once again over the books I'd brought from the library, searching for something which could be read before bed, preferably without blood, or sadistic rituals. I know it's wrong to bring your work home, but for a while, until I got into the topic, it couldn't cause any harm.

I found a promising title, *The Gods' Artefacts– Legends and Untold History.*

I intended to open the book but got interrupted by the loud buzzing of a text message.

"Buy me beer and bring dinner. I'm starving."

Seriously? What happened with 'please'?

I didn't even have the power to get annoyed anymore, he was probably drunk already, anyway. At least, if I got him some more beer, I'd be able to read in peace, without hearing him strumming that out of tune guitar.

Sure, he's supposedly writing a song which will make him famous and filthy rich. I know he can; but in nine months, he hasn't written a single note, yet he'd devour almost ten beers a day–only after, to blame me for our lack of money. Only to say I am the one spending too much. Makes no difference I'm the only one who provides, making sure the bills and rent are paid.

Sometimes I wonder, what happened to the man I fell in love with in the first year of university?

With a swift move, I stuffed the book in my handbag, and I left, shutting the door behind me. Looked like I had shopping to do.

Chapter 2

The smell that struck me when I opened the door to our little apartment almost turned my stomach upside down–cigarette smoke, alcohol, and sweat. I tried to breathe as little as possible until I managed to open the windows, tripping over the empty beer bottles scattered all over the floor.

"Hmph, you're home." I heard a sleepy voice coming from the couch. "Did you get the beer?"

"I'm fine, thanks for asking, and yes, everything is great at work," I said, trying not to be bothered by his lack of interest.

"Yeah, okay, awesome. Now, did you get the fucking beer?" he asked again, losing his patience.

Disgusted, I stepped in front of the couch, throwing the beer cans at him. By the looks of it, that was the only thing he cared for, anyway.

"You got the wrong brand! How can you be so unbelievably fucking stupid?" he raised his voice.

Biting the inside of my cheek, I tried to ignore his insults.

"You could say thank you even for that one."

"Give me some money, and I'll buy it myself. I don't need your help." he puffed.

"Money from where? I haven't been paid yet; I just

started a little while ago. We need to be careful how we spend what we have left, that is, if we don't want to have the surprise of running out of food and rent money.

"Ah, yes," he said, opening a beer. "You and your big and important job at the freaks' museum." He pointed towards me, splashing some beer on the floor. "You weren't even capable of finding a job at a proper museum."

"At least I have one," I responded, trying to keep my calm, which I felt slipping away. "How about you? You promised me you'll look for something, yet you lay on the couch all day long."

"Shut your yap, will ya? Save the theory for someone else." He dismissed my words with a wave. "What's for dinner? And when are you going to clean this place? Just look at the state of this room." He waved around, splashing even more beer on the floor, and on himself.

"Oh, you mean the mess made by you?" I sighed, rubbing my forehead. "You could at least have the decency to clean up after yourself."

I refrained as much as possible not to yell at him. I knew that if a fight started, it wouldn't end until late at night, and I had to get up early in the morning. I threw him the second bag I was holding, with both portions of the Chinese food, and I left for the bedroom, slamming the door behind me. I was tempted to lock it, but it made no difference because he won't come to bed, anyway. In the past few months, the living room couch became an extension of his body. About the same time, he stopped touching me in any way; not even a kiss, nor a kind word, not even the smallest gesture of comforting.

Gradually, I got rid of the dusty work clothes and jumped in the shower. I needed to calm down. I let the hot water wash away all my tiredness and frustrations. The last ten minutes in Jared's company wore me out more than the whole day at the museum. Sometimes, I wonder why I'm still with him. I know for sure that I still love him, but I love Jared from the first six years of our relationship, not the stranger I've been living with for the past nine months.

I met Jared in my first university year. Me, an Arts student, Conservation and Restoration; him, a second year at the Conservatory. The first thing I noticed at him was the way he put his heart into everything he did, and the emotions he transmitted when his fingers touched the piano's keys or the violin's strings. Our relationship developed unhurriedly, and we moved in together after about three years. After we finished our studies, we found jobs wherever we could. Wishing for a life of our own, there was no way we could depend any longer on our parents, who had done their best all those years to support our dreams.

I could say he was a wee bit luckier than me. In a very short time, he found a job as a pianist in a five-star hotel. There, with some help from the manager, he got in contact with a small band at the beginning of the road. Joining the band as a side gig, and with the job at the hotel, he built a name for himself, which became more popular by the day. It didn't take long until they were offered a record signing deal. With all that on his back, he became busier by the day, yet he never once neglected me. He always found time to spend with me, helped me with the housework without waiting for me to ask, he even encouraged me on a steady basis to keep looking for work in my field; he knew very well I was unhappy as a waitress. He never forgot any anniversary or my birthday. Even last year, when I turned twenty-three, he promised me that after they had the first tour, no matter how small, he would propose.

The opportunity showed up two months later. They had to leave in one month, but with a few days before the departure date, Jared suddenly decided he wasn't going anywhere, and he was leaving the band. The only explanation he gave me was that he simply didn't want to and that I shouldn't stick my nose in his decisions. Ever since that night, Jared no longer set foot in the bedroom, spending all his time on the couch in the living room, with a beer in his hand and his eyes glued on the TV screen; occasionally strumming from an out of tune guitar he found at a flea market.

I talked to him countless times, trying to make sense of what was happening with him, but most of those discussions ended up in a fight. All my motivation attempts got lost in thin air, as I talked to the walls. I suggested he take a few counselling sessions, it was a financial effort that I was willing to make without a second thought, but he didn't want to hear about it. The only solution I had left was to stay by his side and hope.

The shower helped me relax, but not enough to help me sleep. I swirled around the room preparing the clothes for the next day. I kicked the handbag I had thrown on the floor, and from it, came the book I'd brought from work. It had completely slipped my mind. I picked it up and carefully opened it to the first page. Under the title, slightly erased was written –Lady Jubilee Conwell. It was rather unusual to find such an old book featuring the original name of the author and not a male penname. The only explanation I could think of, which also made sense, was that there was only one copy of this book, which was created and kept inside the family.

At the bottom of the page, almost impossible to read, was something that looked like a dedication.

"You! The one who does not believe.
Don't shut your eyes to the gifts with which
the gods have endowed you."

It's funny how I, the one who didn't believe, was reading this message. But I couldn't help but wonder who it was really for. I set the book on the nightstand until I finished the rest of the preparations for the following day; just in time to hear some heavy snoring coming from the living room. I didn't want to leave the room under any circumstances, but my heart wouldn't allow me to let him sleep in the cold, with the window open and without a blanket. Sliding the door open, I passed by Jared on the tip of my toes, closed the window, covered him with a blanket, and turned the TV off. It seemed his light went off after only half a beer but looking at the pile of empty cans and bottles from around the couch, I could say he had far exceeded his norm.

Once back in the bedroom, I jumped in bed. Sure, it was a bit too early to go to sleep, but there was no reason for me not to enjoy the silence and read for a while; after all, this was the initial plan.

Picking up the book, I opened it with care. I had to be very careful with it since it was so old. Perhaps I could strengthen it a bit at work, I didn't want to have a surprise as it unravelled between my fingers. As old as it was, there was no table of contents, but there was a short introduction, similar to a letter for someone.

"It blisses my weakened soul that after such a long time, this book has finally come in your possession. I know you do not believe now, but what awaits you in the near future will turn your life upside down, and just by opening your eyes and having faith in the unseen world around you, you will be able to overcome the challenges that will mark your destiny.

The Artefacts about which you will read in the following pages, affected the world in different ways, both good and bad. I do realise the list is far from complete. Some of them have disappeared entirely from the surface of the Earth, leaving behind only legends, while the ones that still exist are mainly inoffensive; except for one which has the power to ruin any life that comes in contact with it.

I know you will have many questions for me, and I will try to answer them all, as accurately as I can when we meet.

I hope to see you soon, and when I do, I hope you will believe."

I somehow felt as if that letter was meant for me. The context was spot on. My life was messed up, and I unquestionably didn't believe, but the meeting part was out of the question since the author and I existed in different centuries.

I turned the pages, reading the chapters' titles. They were pretty obvious–Aphrodite's Heart, Zeus's Lightning, Poseidon's Pearl, Artemis's Bow, and so on. The drawings were quite suggestive, and one or two looked somewhat familiar.

Just a strange coincidence.

I kept turning the pages until I reached a missing portion. Someone was either excessively brutal with the book and didn't bother to put back the escaping pieces of paper, or they didn't want for this bit to be read. There were twenty missing pages; a chapter, or maybe two, since on the next page a new one began. I'm not sure why I felt sorry for that, but there was nothing I could do, so I returned to the first chapter and began to read.

I found it very interesting that she chose the first chapter to be about Aphrodite and her artefact and not about Zeus, who was *the god* among gods. As I read through the rows, I became more and more captivated. I remember what a pleasure it was for me, as a child, to learn about gods, heroes, mythological creatures, and their legends. Looked like nothing really had changed since then. Lady Jubilee had an extraordinarily clear storytelling style, with no detours but without skipping over important points.

Aphrodite's Heart was a precious stone which brought its bearer fame, admiration, and respect, being infused with the very essence of the Love Goddess. It was one of the few artefacts still intact, at least at that time, being relatively inoffensive. For an extended period, the stone could be found in possession of the Royal Family, as one of the crown's jewels.

In time, it was in hands who had no clue about its power, but there also existed those who abused it. The result was a temporary energy exhaustion; the moment in which everyone under its influence turned against the bearer, sometimes leading to death.

Unfortunately, I had to close the book, too scared

not to break it. Every time I turned a page, the spine crackled loudly. With the feeling I'd be swamped starting the next day, I tried to go to sleep. Actually, it was more the email I got from the Director than my intuition. Something about an assemblage which had to be prepared for display ASAP. No more details were added, but something told me this would turn into overtime.

Oh, well, at least I'm paid for it.

I was more tired than I thought. I fell asleep the moment my head touched the pillow and woke up due to that infuriating alarm clock. It was time to get ready for work, but I didn't have any longing to get out of bed. I moved around stealthily, having no intention of waking up Jared and giving him the chance to ruin my day so early in the morning. The last thing I had to do before leaving was to get the book. If I was going to finish it, I had to strengthen it.

The book, which I had carefully placed closed on the nightstand, was now opened at the missing pages.

Chapter 3

And . . . I was right.

The assemblage the Director mentioned, was, in fact, a massive collection of runes, tarot cards, and bones, used for future readings. The only way to finish all this by the deadline was to work overtime. The idea delighted and frightened me at the same time; delighted by the extra money coming my way at the end of the month and frightened by the possibility of staying all by myself in that place.

With a soft knock on the door, Laura came in, flashing a smile.

"I came to say goodbye."

"You're leaving?" I asked, a bit disappointed.

"The shift is over; the museum is closed. You should go home soon as well."

"I'll try, but these pieces are so meticulous that it takes me ages, and the Director wants at least half of them by Friday."

"He is worse than a slave driver sometimes." She scowled, putting her hands on her hips. "Try not to exhaust yourself, though. Your health is more important than whatever His Highness might say."

"I'll try." I giggled. "I promise not to stay for more than another two hours." But despite my promise, I didn't realise when the time passed, and soon the grand clock in the main hall struck midnight.

This can't be happening! I said to myself, but as fictional as I wished it to be, it was the truth, which meant the only option left to get home was by taxi; an expense I was unwilling to make.

I quickly checked the time on my phone. Midnight, indeed, yet not even a call or text from Jared. I bet he didn't even notice my absence. His concern certainly warmed my heart.

There was no point in heading home now. Also, if I were to take a taxi, it would still take about thirty-forty minutes. I would be left with only a few hours to sleep and would also waste money I didn't have.

I made a little space on the desk, folded my scarf and put my head on it. I knew I'd wake up with back pain, but despite my uncomfortable position, I fell asleep.

As I fell asleep, I heard, closer and closer, the ticking of a clock. In that darkness, a young woman approached me, with a pocket watch wrapped around her right arm.

"I've been waiting for you for so long, and you're finally here," she said hopefully before she vanished.

When I opened my eyes, I felt my soul breaking in half. These weren't my feelings, but they were just as painful. In front of my teary eyes stood an older woman with chestnut hair tied in a loop at the back of her head, a few wrinkles here and there, and eyes filled with compassion. She seemed nice, but that didn't make me feel any better. I could hear other people talking around me; about money, about something they sold, but it made no sense to me. I couldn't understand what was happening. Another woman lowered to my level and tried to speak calmly, stroking my head and hair, while her eyes were full of tears.

"I know this is difficult for you, but think about your brothers and sisters. If we hadn't done this, they would've starved to death. You know mama loves you no matter what."

"If that were true, you wouldn't have sold me like an animal," a child's voice was heard.

It was me, but I had no control over what I said or did. I was a spectator through someone else's eyes. Right at that moment, a firm slap hit the child's face, throwing her to the ground, and a man—the father, I presumed—grabbed the mother by the arm and dragged her away. The woman who until then had just sat on the side and watched, came near the child who had risen in the meantime.

"Don't worry, you will see your family again," she tried to encourage her. "The Earl and his family are very kind people. My name is Emma, and I will teach you everything you need to know, so you will have a good life working in this house."

She nodded.

"What's your name, child?" Emma asked.

"L-Leah," she answered among sighs.

"Follow me, Leah. We need to get you cleaned up and fix your uniform, but first, you need to eat something; you're nothing but skin and bones."

Leah had never seen so much food in her life, and maybe, if it were an ordinary day, she would have enjoyed the plate in front of her, but her parents had given her away from home for less money than you could take on a lamb.

The grey dress, which served as her uniform, was a little loose, but she had never received a new dress *nor* had a dress that would be hers alone, without having to share it with her sisters. A ray of hope began to sprout in her soul. Maybe this wasn't going to be so bad after all. All the other servants she met along the way, encouraged her as much as they could, though they had never seen her before, and all had nothing to say but words of praise when it came to the Earl's family.

"Leah, come with me," Emma said. "The young lady wants to meet you."

I felt her soul shiver with fear. What if she would say something stupid? What if the young lady wouldn't like her, and she would drive her away? She began to walk scared, with her eyes on the floor, one step behind Emma who started to educate her.

"Remember the first and most essential rule. Never talk without being talked to first; never make direct eye contact unless requested, and you respect all orders no matter how strange they might sound. You will see in time that they are exceptional people with very peculiar interests. And one more thing; in this house, gossiping is not allowed under any circumstances.

It wasn't long before they stopped in front of two big, white doors. After a short knock, from the other side, a crystalline voice was heard.

"Come on in, Emma."

She pushed the heavy doors, and both entered the spacious room.

"My Lady, I brought her. This is Lady Jubilee Conwell;" Emma addressed the child. "After you learn what you have to do, you will take care of her quarters and fulfil any orders you may receive from her ladyship."

Leah attempted something like a clumsy reverence, but then, curiosity overcame her fear, and raising her eyes slightly from the floor, Leah looked at the woman in whose hands was laying her fate. As she looked up, we were more and more enchanted by what we saw; starting from the blue dress so elaborately made, the long black hair falling in waves reaching down to her hips, white skin, and black eyes with thick eyelashes...

"You are so beautiful," Leah said aloud; but realising her mistake, she quickly averted her eyes, ashamed.

She'd been there for less than five minutes and already broken a rule. Closing her eyes tightly, she waited for her punishment, but Lady Jubilee only chuckled.

"Raise your face, child," she said. "What is your name?"

"Leah, my Lady," she answered, slightly lifting her

head, only to notice that the distance between the two of them was only getting smaller.

"You are so tiny." Her eyes narrowed. "How old are you?"

"Thirteen."

"Emma, it is your responsibility to make sure from now on Leah is fed properly. In her current state, she won't even be able to lift a pillow."

"Yes, my Lady." Emma bowed her head.

"I know I can count on you to do what's right. You are a strong young woman," she said, placing a hand on the child's chest, "and you will get even stronger with proper guidance. You and I will get along just fine." She smiled.

Lady Jubilee looked her deep in the eyes, but it was like she could see something beyond Leah. It was as if she could see me.

I woke up with a bang when my behind touched the floor. Maybe it would be a good idea, if I'll ever have slumber parties at work again, to lock the chair's wheels before going to sleep.

I got back on my feet with some difficulty, rubbing the painful area. That's what I got for not paying attention to my surroundings. And speaking of surroundings, the sun was up in the sky and had been for quite a while, but why was it so quiet?

I went out to the empty and quiet museum. Even the main doors were locked, and there was a perfectly reasonable explanation for it; it was Monday. The museum was always closed on Mondays, so I could go home. I slapped my forehead; I could've gone home last night. At least now I could use the monthly ticket and not waste any more money. I went back to my workshop to collect my things, and I would have almost left without the book if the cream pages on my desk hadn't caught my eye. I was quite sure I'd left it closed; yet, again, it was opened at the missing pages. Maybe I hit it with my hand during the night. I took it to put it in my bag, but stopped mid-way; had I just had a dream about Lady Jubilee? What meant a tired mind; so easily influenced.

It was time to go, I needed sleep in a proper bed.

The way back home was at the very least exhausting. As usual, the underground was so crowded, that if someone was moving, even an inch, I could have kissed the neck of the person in front of me. No wonder I had no social life, spending time with humans was draining.

Finally getting in front of the door, I wished only for silence. And it really was quiet; there was no music, no television, not a sound of Jared's alcohol-induced snoring; nothing at all.

Opening the door, I stepped into the empty

apartment. To my surprise, he was nowhere to be seen. Maybe he left to look for a job; perhaps our life was finally returning to normal. On my way to the bedroom, I abandoned my clothes wherever I could. Finally giving up on my underwear, I slipped between the soft sheets before sleep snatched me before I could even count to ten.

I could hear the pocket-watch's ticking again. There was something relaxing about that symmetric sound. My head rested in someone's lap; they caressed my hair, humming a lullaby. It didn't sound familiar, but it felt so pleasant. I opened my eyes and saw stars. Millions and millions of stars shone around us. The lullaby stopped, but in exchange, that person talked to me softly.

"Don't be scared; the disappointment will leave, and love will return to you soon. Rest now, the way ahead is far from easy. I will need your help, but you're not ready yet. Rest now, but time goes fast without looking back. I know you don't believe now, but we need you. Soon, you will meet again the one that I was once. Tell her to go straight to Lady Jubilee; she knows what needs to be done. Scarlett, are you listening?"

"Yes," I answered sleepily.

"You need to hear a story from her. I know the pages are missing, but she doesn't, because that happened a good while after she was gone. So many sleepless nights, so much wasted energy to gather all the information in that book, and even so. . .. It breaks my heart knowing he is still alive, and it's all my fault."

"Who?"

"You will find out at some point. If I tell you now, everything shall be destroyed. You will have to believe, Scarlett. Without your faith, all hope will be lost. Maybe if I were stronger, I could've stopped him, and saved everyone, but it's too late for me. Open your eyes, and you'll see," her voice was calm, but there was an urgency in the way she talked.

"I . . . I'll try."

"Good. Now sleep tight. I missed you so much all these years, my dear friend."

It was almost dark when I opened my eyes. I felt so at peace as I hadn't been in a long time. My stomach was asking for its rights, and most certainly, I needed a bath, probably smelling like the museum's exhibits. I got dressed quickly and headed for the small kitchen, but stopped in my path, instead, when I opened the bedroom's sliding door. It was quiet, and it was dark. I was still home alone. I was going to wait a little while longer before I called Jared, though maybe I shouldn't even do it. After all, he hadn't called me when I missed a whole night from home. Bet he didn't even notice, much less worry. But I *did* notice and couldn't help it. I got my phone and called him three times; each time it rang once then I got redirected to the voice mail. He rejected my calls. I tried to call him again a few minutes later, but he turned it off. There was nothing to be worried about. No; more likely, there was no one to be concerned about.

After another twenty long minutes, Jared entered

through the door, and he had company. A step behind him, a young woman; blonde, tall, and slim—the
type who could effortlessly make a modelling career,
but through some unconventional methods. Neither
of them spared me a glance. Got in fast, grabbed a
suitcase prepared beforehand, and left without looking back. He pushed the keys through the mail slot,
acting like I wasn't even there. Probably that was the
plan; get in, grab the stuff, and get out while I wasn't
home. And now I was alone, again, trying to wrap my
head around what just happened.

Somehow, it shouldn't surprise me. For anyone
else, it was as clear as daylight the direction in which
our relationship had been headed for some time, I
guess I was the only one who had my hopes up. But
even so, I felt something strange, as if for the first
time in forever, I could breathe. He was gone, and I
wasn't sorry. Maybe laughing wasn't the most natural
reaction, but that's what I did; I laughed. A burst of
hysterical laughter which gradually turned into crying. The irony? I wasn't crying over him, but for all the
time I wasted waiting for him to get back to normal.

What an idiot I've been.

But now it was over, and I felt free. Despite all the
beautiful years spent together, in the end, he turned
out to be nothing but a big disappointment, but it was
okay. No one could ever take away all the beautiful
memories, and the bad ones I could bury them in a
hidden corner of my mind, just like every time before.

Chapter 4

Two months came and passed, a period which I spent mostly at the museum. I had more than enough work to do, so little to no time left to worry about anything else. I even made a habit of coming here on Mondays, when it was closed and spend the day reading in the library. Curiously, I became more and more interested in the book's topics.

Time rolled, and it was Monday again. I really didn't want to stay home, but I had so much to do – shopping, cleaning, maybe even some cooking since I was already tired of the food from the fast-food from across the street. Take all that and add an emergency beauty salon visit. My hair was all over the place, and my hands, couldn't even look at them. Perhaps all the chemicals I was working with protected the exhibits, but my nails couldn't stand them very much, despite wearing protective gloves.

Everything took less time than expected. The cleaning was a breeze since there was no one around to make a mess in the first place. Shopping; a real pleasure, buying only the things I like, after all, I didn't need to share them with anyone. At the beauty salon, things got a bit complicated. My hair was in such a condition that it needed a stronger, time consuming, and pricier treatment, but it was alright. I had all the time in the world, and the money was all mine.

Feeling relaxed, beautiful, and very tired, I finally got home, and unpacking the groceries, put them each into their place. In a very hidden corner, in a cupboard, I found concealed, a sparkling wine bottle, which I'd completely forgotten about. I got it a while ago for a special occasion, but today was as good of a time as any other day. Today marked two months since Jared vanished from my life, and I felt better than ever. Popping it open, I poured a glass while I prepared dinner, and another two after, but maybe the last one was a bit too much. I wasn't used to drinking alcohol, but because of the sweet, subtle aroma, I couldn't tell when it became too much; that is, until I got up from my chair.

Did I spin, or was it the room?

I set my destination for the bed.

The early evening hour didn't matter anymore thanks to my special bottle. Leaning against furniture and walls, I managed to reach the bedroom and the bed, safely. I had only one wish left; to not feel sick the next day at work. I fell asleep almost instantly. Who needs sleeping pills when you have wine for dinner?

I was floating again among the stars. There was something about that place, something soothing, but why was I alone? The last time there was another person with me.

"Is anyone here?" I shouted.

"I'm here, Scarlett. Don't be afraid," a calm voice answered, but my eyes couldn't find her.

"Where are you? I can't see you."

"Listen for the watch's ticking, that's how you'll find me."

Closing my eyes, I listened. At first, I couldn't hear a thing, but little by little, the sound became stronger until it appeared as if it came from next to me. And it was. The young woman, with the pocket watch tied around her right forearm, was standing right by my side, watching me with a warm smile.

I looked at her, curious.

What detailed dreams I had, though I couldn't remember ever being so aware in a dream before. I could see even the smallest details of the cinnamon-coloured dress she was wearing. The tailoring seemed to belong to the 19th century, and the material looked fairly expensive.

The short-sleeved design made me think about the evening dresses worn at various social events, but her hair, like cappuccino foam, was only partially tied with a bow, the same colour as the dress, on top of the head, the rest of it falling down her shoulders. A hairstyle way too simple and childish for someone her age. Her white skin looked as if it never saw the sun, and the big, grey eyes were shadowed by sadness. She was gorgeous. No; she was outstanding, but dreaming her made me obsessed with the period she was coming from?

"What is this place? Where are we?" I asked, looking around at the countless stars.

"We are outside Time, inside Chronos's heart.

"What strange dreams I have," I said laughing.

"You still don't believe," she added, saddened.

"Believe in what?"

"In what happens around you, but you refuse to open your eyes."

"Nothing is going on around me." I rolled my eyes.

"Then what do you call this? What do you call this place?" She spread her arms and turned once, her dress fluttering around her legs. "What do you call our meeting?" she asked, nervous.

"A dream."

"But it's not a dream, Scarlett. What do you need to believe?" she asked, disappointed.

"Proof. How can I believe in something I can't see?"

"How strange," she puffed, leaving out a bitter laugh. "You never struck me as a naive person. You want proof? Very well. Tomorrow, Laura will guide around the museum a group of children. At one point, a boy, the smallest one in the group, will ask her to exemplify a quick chant. I want you to look for the aura that will appear around her. You can ask her about it later on. She will be more than happy to share her secret with you."

"What makes you so sure? If it's a secret, wouldn't it be more logical for her to keep it to herself?"

"Scarlett," she talked like to a stubborn child. "She

knows you are special, and she wants to help you, she just doesn't know how to approach you about this."

"Look, I know she looks like a witch most of the time, but that doesn't mean she is one."

She lingered for a while after hearing my answer.

"If this is not enough evidence for you, then there's one more thing. In the library, on the fourth shelf of the oldest bookshelf, is a secret compartment. You will find a letter which is addressed to you, but you can't read it yet."

"Let's say, for the love of this conversation, that I'll find the letter, though I highly doubt it since all this is *just a dream*. Why shouldn't I read it since it's mine?"

"Because first, you need to meet the person who wrote it," she said calmly.

"But why is that so important?" I asked, losing my patience.

"Because it will remain the only person we can rely on when everyone else turns their back on us," she continued.

"Us?" I asked distrustfully, raising an eyebrow.

"Us."

"Okay, I'm really starting to think it was a bad idea to drink that wine."

Suddenly, an ear-piercing alarm began to ring louder and louder, causing me an intense headache.

"What the hell is this?" I shouted, covering my ears with the palms of my hands.

"Time for you to go."

The young woman came closer to me and put her right hand on my head. Only then I noticed. The watch's chain, which I thought wrapped around her forearm, came out from under her skin, making them one.

"Wait!" I yelled. "You never told me who you are!"

"But you already know that, Scarlett."

With her arm still extended at the level of my head, she swiftly moved away, and I woke up shouting her name.

"Leah!"

Chapter 5

I felt like someone had run me over with a truck filled with massive wood furniture.

That's it! Whatever's left in the wine bottle from last night will go straight down the drain. That if I manage to get out of bed without ruining the carpet.

"Oh, my head . . ." Though not undeserved. "I don't want to work today."

I covered my face with a pillow, trying to hide from the cruel reality in which I had to abandon my comfortable bed and get ready to face the outside world.

"Come on, Scarlett, you can do this," I tried to encourage myself. "Just go in the workshop and hide between books. You don't have to talk to anybody or pay them any attention. You just have to move your feet. Ugh, why am I talking to myself?" I whined into the pillow.

I must've used half the energy I had just to get out of bed and head to the bathroom. I, indeed, felt slightly better after a warmish shower, but the headache just didn't leave me alone. The way to the museum appeared to be the longest in my life, even though, to get to my parents was an eight-hour long train ride.

I managed to get in my workshop without bumping

into anyone on the way, now I had to keep doing it for the rest of the day, and I was going to be fine. I let my head rest on the desk's cold surface, but when I closed my eyes, Leah's saddened face appeared in my mind out of nowhere.

It's just a dream, so cut the nonsense.

And I was going to prove it to myself. There was no way I could stalk Laura to see if she was doing magic tricks for kids and look for God-knows-what aura around her; that was way too weird. But my presence in the library was something completely natural. I strolled all the way to the library, paying attention to any movement around me. I was in no mood for chatting.

Finding the oldest bookshelf was far from a challenge since it clearly was the one from the 16th century, and the fourth shelf, obviously packed with books. I removed them carefully, and what did I see? There was nothing out of the ordinary. It was just a dream.

Now, perhaps if I weren't intoxicated from the night before, I would've noticed faster that the pattern on the back of said shelf, didn't match the rest. The difference was tiny, challenging to see without proper lighting; but it was there.

Nope, no way. There was no fricking way. I was just paranoid. There was no way my dream could be more than that. Those kind of things just didn't exist. I removed the books from the next shelf. The two should've matched, and that would've been enough proof that my mind was playing a prank on me and everything was as usual as it should be, but they didn't. I ended up clearing all the shelves, only to have a big surprise; all matched, except for the fourth one.

"Alright, Scarlett. Keep calm. There surely is a perfectly plausible explanation for this."

Maybe at some point, it needed some repairs done, and this was where the difference came from. That sounded reasonable, but then why I wasn't convinced? I needed to prove to myself that this was nothing but a regular bookshelf, without any secrets, and then go back to my work. Also, I had to stop talking out loud to myself.

I had to think logically. If there was, indeed, a secret compartment, then inside, should be air. In which case, if I knocked in different spots, I should hear dissimilar noises. I tapped the back of the shelf on all its length; no difference. What made me try on a different one, I'll never understand, but when the noises didn't sound alike, I knocked a little bit harder. I was simultaneously tapping on both shelves, but no matter how much I tried, they didn't match, and they were never going to.

Behind the fake wooden panel was something I couldn't know about; I *shouldn't* know about. I tried to shove my nails by the false back, push it upward, downward, and sideways. Nothing; it was unmovable. And maybe it would've stayed that way if a little, bothered spider wouldn't have come out from behind the panel, through a tiny hole in the bottom, left corner.

Too small to fit my finger in it, but just about right for one of my hairpins. I pushed it in until it clicked, and when I pulled it out, the panel fell. Trapped in spider webs, an envelope with my name on it was waiting. I managed to extract it without causing a baby spider genocide. They looked cute when small enough to barely see them.

I set the panel back in its place and quickly re-arranged the books, sure, the order was different, but at least they were off of the floor. The letter, which was now in my pocket, gave me an extraordinary state of discomfort, or maybe it was mostly from the hang-over, I couldn't say for sure. The red-wax seal was intact, and my name was clearly written on the front of the envelope. I was tempted to open it, but then I remembered something else. If the letter was real, then Laura was actually a witch?

I left the library behind, running. In my rush to-wards the museum's main hall, I almost knocked poor Matteo off his feet. He got away unharmed, but some of the papers he held, fell on the floor.

"Sorry, Matteo!" I shouted back, but I didn't stop to help him. I had somewhere I had to be.

Coincidently, or not, Laura did have a group of chil-dren today; scouts. I met them just as they entered the last room of the tour. I couldn't bother them, but there was no real reason why I couldn't follow them around.

"This exhibition is called *The Forest's Nymphs*," she started talking to the eager group.

This was the first time I saw Laura working, and it was clear she enjoyed what she was doing.

"Were they real nymphs?" asked one of the boys.

"No. They were not. They were humans; witches."

"Then why were they called nymphs?" asked another.

"Because they helped as much as they could. At that time, people believed that all magic practitioners handled dark magic, that they were the devil's pawns. So, whenever they met a white magic witch, they confused her for a nymph. In their minds, anyone who used magic to help another couldn't be human, and that only the daughters of the forest had healing abilities."

"And how were they healing? By boiling potions out of toad eyes?" joked one of the mothers.

"Yes, and no," Laura answered, laughing. "They used in equal measure enchantments and potions, but not out of toad's eyes, instead out of medicinal herbs."

"Do you know any spells?"

"I know a few."

"Can you show us one?"

At first, I couldn't see who asked the last question but as the other boys moved, in front came a carroty-haired boy; the smallest one in the group.

"Sure, I can, love. But only one, and I'll make it on my colleague. Looks like she had a rough night and might need one.

I was taken by surprise when she pointed at me.

While the kids looked confused, the mothers start giggling.

"How do you know what sort of night I had?" I asked jokingly.

"It's written all over your face, sweets. Now come here."

She motioned me to a small chair in a corner. With so many curious looks pointed at me, I decided it was best to close my eyes. I could feel Laura moving around me. I tried my best not to snicker when she started making some strange noises, but then I heard them; hidden from other's ears, the echo of some words. Was it Latin? Ancient Greek? Or maybe a dialect lost hundreds of years ago. Bewildered by the peace those unknown words offered me, I opened my eyes. Laura, who looked as if she was dancing around me, gave off a light which environed us both. It pulsed in waves and changing colours, looking like the Aurora Borealis shining in the northern skies.

Was I the only one seeing this?

No.

Judging by the looks of some of the children, they could perceive it as well, even if only a small part of what I could see.

The show ended with ovations; my headache disappeared completely, and after the end of the tour, the group headed towards the gift shop, where Silvia had to take over the kids' question rush.

"Let's get a coffee," she said with an understanding smile.

I followed Laura to the staff kitchenette, where she prepared two cups of coffee, then we retreated to my workshop.

"So, you believe now?" she asked, leaning on the edge of the desk.

"I'm not sure what to believe anymore. What will I find out next? That Hogwarts is a real school?"

"Sadly, no. Such a school would've been beneficial. There are a lot of children, who as they grow up, develop all sorts of more or less dangerous talents. Some of them pass through life without even noticing, while others can't live with them, often ending up in tragedy."

"What about you? Laura, are you really a . . .?" I couldn't bring myself to finish the sentence.

"Although I'm not very fond of the word—sounds malicious—yes, I'm a witch."

"I don't get it. How it happened?" I asked puzzled.

"In my case, it's inherited through blood, and I'm quite sure it's the same for you."

"Me?" I raised an eyebrow.

"Yup. I can't tell for sure what you can do, but I know you have a lot of potential. I have an idea," she said, excited. "Let's make a test."

"What test?" I asked cautiously.

"Just wait here for a bit. It's nothing to be scared of, I promise."

Laura left the room for a few minutes, then returned holding a painting.

"Well? What do you think?" she placed the painting in front of me.

"Is that Beethoven?" I asked, unsure of where all this was going.

"Give it a second. Just look at it carefully."

"Why do I have the feeling he's looking back at me?"

"Wait . . ."

"Did he just wink at me?" I moved slightly back as if he was about to jump out any second.

"Oh, he likes you!" Laura said, thrilled.

"And now he blew me a kiss," I said a bit creeped out. "What's wrong with this painting? Where are the batteries?"

"It doesn't have any, but I'm surprised by his reaction. Usually, he makes scary faces, which is why we had to take him off the walls. Poor Gregor almost had a heart attack."

I snorted, covering my mouth with one hand.

"It's not funny," Laura scolded me.

"Yes, it is. He just stuck his tongue out at you."

It was hard for me to stop laughing when such a stoic character made all kinds of silly faces at Laura.

"So, what's his story?" I asked, wiping away a tear from the corner of my eye.

"It's quite a simple one," she answered, placing the painting on the side. "He stole the wrong person's heart, and in fact, it wasn't even him, but his music."

"In that painting . . . it's really his spirit?"

"Not at all. The woman couldn't retain her burning desire, so she fully transposed it on to this canvas."

"Desire? Sounds more like an obsession to me."

"Maybe, but that's not how it ended up like this" she pointed to the painting. "She, like many others, had no idea what she was capable of, so she kept living her life as normal. The painting, on the other hand, still in her possession, absorbed more and more of her power, and in time, came to life."

"There must be a lot of such strange cases all over the world." My eyes widened.

"Oh, you have no idea, but I find something curious. You are the first person who he didn't try to scare off".

"Who knows? Maybe I'm his type." I giggled. "But what about you? Seems to me like you get along just fine."

"Nah; he tried to scare me plenty of times, but I told him if he did it one more time, I'd drop him accidentally in a fire, and then he stopped."

"Laura, can I ask you something?" I fidgeted. "But it needs to remain between you and me."

"Sure, you can, sweets. What's on your mind?"

"I've had these strange dreams lately, with a young woman who keeps saying she waited for me and that she needs my help."

"And why don't you help her?"

"I don't know how." I squeezed the empty cup in my hands.

"In that case, next time you dream her, ask her to show you. I'm sure she will, but if I were you, I would try to find out as much as possible. Spirits know things far beyond our wildest imagination. Okay, need to go now. The next group will arrive soon."

"Thank you, Laura. It means a lot to me to be able to talk to someone about all this." I smiled.

"Anytime," she smiled back at me and left.

What scared me the most had happened. I believed. Maybe if I would've witnessed only Laura's powers, I would have found an explanation; the light's angle, or something similar. But, in my pocket, I had the incontestable proof that a world beyond the tips of my fingers existed. A world I was part of but still denied it entirely.

I couldn't do that anymore.

Chapter 6

The following days passed as peacefully as they could, which turned out to be damn frustrating. Now, when I believed, when I found the letter, when I witnessed Laura's spells, not to mention that weird Beethoven portrait, I didn't get any sign from Leah.

Nothing.

I believed, goddamn it.

Perhaps she couldn't contact me whenever she wanted to, but maybe the other way around was possible as well, yet I had no idea how these things worked. What was I supposed to do? Spiritualism? Pray to the stars? Hmm, Mayan incantations? What?

Still at work, I didn't want my colleagues to think I was crazy, but perhaps I had to act like one at least partially, so I started shouting as loudly as I could . . . in my mind.

"I believe now! Can you hear me, Leah? Now I believe, so what more do you want from me? Leah!"

I wasn't waiting for an answer really, but I did feel a bit more relaxed.

"Who are you?"

Was it just me, or did I hear something? I stopped everything I was doing, and closing my eyes, I kept listening, focusing on any sound no matter how small; but the silence extended.

"*Can you hear me?*"

At the sound of her voice, my eyes flew open, but I couldn't see my desk anymore. I was somewhere outside, where two nimble hands hung a bunch of freshly washed clothes to dry.

"*Yes, I can,*" I answered a bit disordered.

"*Who are you? I know we've met before, but I don't know who you are.*"

"*When have we met?*" I pried.

"*When I was thirteen, on the same day my parents left me here. I felt I wasn't alone. I felt you, but I couldn't say back then for sure.*"

"*And I thought it was all a dream.*"

"*Are you my guardian angel?*" she asked, curious.

"*No, sorry. I'm just a regular human.*"

"*Then how is it possible for me to talk to you, though you're not next to me? Am I going mad?*"

"*No, you're not, and I can't explain it, either. It's just as new for me as it is for you, but what happens now still doesn't feel real to me.*"

"*But it is. This is the world I live in. What about you? Where are you from?*" her interest spiked.

"*Wait. Let's take things slowly. I am Scarlett, and you must be Leah.*"

"*Yes, that's right,*" she said, amazed.

"*How old are you now?*"

"*Seventeen.*"

"And do you know what year it is?"

"It's 1835."

"So, 19th century." I said more to myself.

"Now tell me about you and your world," she requested excited.

"My world is in the future, in 2019, and I am twenty-four years old."

She was so amazed, but I didn't have time to let her get a grip. I could feel her curiosity growing, but I needed to meet Jubilee.

"Leah, listen! You need to go to Lady Jubilee and tell her about me."

"But I can't," she said, scared. *"She'll think I've lost my sanity."*

"She won't because she knows I've been here before. The first time you two met, she somehow could tell I was there as well, and I have reasons to believe she's expecting me. There must be a motive behind our connection, and I think she can help us find it. It might have something to do with her book."

"You mean the one about the Gods' Artefacts?"

"Yes. I need you to take me to her."

We went straight for her quarters without taking any detours. She didn't even manage to knock on the door before, from the other side, we heard a voice.

"Come on in, Leah."

Despite the vast social status difference, her tone was friendly and kind, far from authoritarian.

"How did she know it was you?"

"I don't know, but she does it every time."

"I am sorry to bother you, but–" Leah stepped in the room.

"Finally, you're here," Jubilee interrupted her.

"Forgive me my Lady, were you waiting for me?"

"Leah, listen to me carefully. I need to talk to your guest, but to do so, you'll need to give her temporary control over your body."

"But I don't know how to do that," she said fearfully, her eyes widening.

"Just close your eyes, breathe in, and imagine pushing her in front," Jubilee explained calmly.

Leah did that precisely. Closing her eyes, she breathed in deeply and pushed me. I felt tingling throughout the body as I gained control, but I was worried. What if I couldn't change back?

"Leah?"

"I'm here."

"I've been waiting for you for a while. Please have a seat. Would you like some tea and cookies?"

I sat on a chair in front of her. On the table next to us, was a plate with all sorts of mini-cakes and cookies, and a pot with freshly made tea, but I couldn't care less about those. I had to learn more.

"How did you know about me; back then, and even today?"

"Just like you, and Leah," she said, pouring me a cup of tea, and one for herself. "I was born with a rather unusual talent. While other young ladies spent their days playing the piano or cross-stitching, I looked for answers for past problems in the future. I looked for diverse objects and followed them across history, witnessing their fate, how they affected human life, and sometimes, even how they were destroyed," she explained.

"That sounds amazing," I said, impressed, reaching for a cake.

"It is, but it came with a price no one could tell me about. By abusing my talent, my body suffered, and I noticed too late. I'm afraid my time is quite limited now, and although I gave up on my journeys, at times, I'm pulled into the flow without me wanting to."

"I'm . . . sorry."

"Don't be. It was my choice. A bad one, but mine alone." She smiled.

I could see, even without her telling me that something was wrong. The first time I saw her, she was radiant, but now looked pale and prematurely aged. While Jubilee seemed to be at peace with the near-end, I could feel the pain in Leah's heart. In the past few years, she grew to care genuinely for her, and she was going to leave her soon.

"I need to ask you about the book. First, can you tell me who are the dedication and letter at the very beginning for?" I asked, changing the subject.

"For you." She sipped from her cup.

"But . . . how did you know it would get to me?" I was confused.

"I followed my family's evolution, and that's how I found you."

"But what is it you want from me? What can I possibly do?" I frowned.

"For a start, to tell me if you read it."

"I did, apart from the broken pages."

"What broken pages?" she scowled.

"Give me a second," I said, tapping with my finger on the wooden table. "I think it was from Athena's Feather to Hera's Veil if I remember correctly."

"Chronos's Watch," she pinched the bridge of her nose, grimacing. "I should've imagined."

"'Chronos's Watch'? What is that?" I asked, not understanding her reaction.

"It's one of the first created artefacts, and also the one our family is supposed to protect."

"Oh," was the only thing I could say.

"The legend I know was transmitted from one generation to another in our family, but I can't tell how accurate it is. After Chronos ate his children and realised Rhea hid Zeus, he went searching for him."

"Yes, I know the legend. He can't find him, but Zeus returns after he grows up and wipes the floor with him," I said impatiently, causing Jubilee to giggle due to my choice of words.

"That is what everyone knows," she said after a short while. "But what is unknown, it that in his hunt, Chronos fell for a mortal woman. While it's true he had Rhea for a wife, he didn't care about her. He wanted Calia by his side. Aware of the mortal's fragility and short lifespan, Chronos created the Watch by ripping out a piece of his own heart. The Watch had the power to give Calia eternal life, but Rhea was possessive and vengeful. She cursed the Watch, so anyone who uses it is able to live only by gradually consuming the lives from those around them. Fortunately, Calia was wise enough to not use the artefact, and with an effort which almost cost her life, she completely sealed both the powers of the Watch and its curse."

"How did she know she couldn't use it?" I asked, engrossed in her story.

"Calia, just like her mother, and grandmother before them had the clairvoyance gift. She knew well the price she would have to pay, but was unwilling to make such sacrifices, because the first affected would've been her family."

"There's one thing I don't understand." I shrugged.

"What is it?"

"Why did you want me to know about this artefact in particular? If it's under your family's protection, then everything should be fine, right?

"If only it were that simple. Unfortunately, that's far from the truth. Someone will break the rules and attempt to break the seals," she explained, saddened, and a bit ashamed.

"Can it be undone so effortlessly?" I asked, alarmed.

"No. It requires a lot of work and a special talent, but in time, and with a lot of effort, he will succeed."

"Who?" I pry.

"My father," Jubilee responded with a sad smile.

"After I'm gone, he will most likely lose his mind and stop being the man he is now. Everyone around him will suffer, yet I can't do a thing to stop him."

Looking at my hands resting on my knees, I kept quiet for a while, trying to absorb all the information.

"You said that both I, and Leah have special talents." I raised my head, looking into her eyes. "For me, it's becoming quite clear what that is, but what about Leah?"

"The fact that your souls resonate to such a level that you were capable of breaking the time barrier, is nothing but a tiny part of what both of you can do."

"Then what can I do?"

"I'm afraid I can't tell you that; at least not until you know who you are. The rest, Leah will tell you in time."

"Leah?"

"I don't know what she's talking about," Leah answered just as confused as me.

"I apologise. Leah doesn't know, either, but she will find out in the future."

"Alright, don't tell me," I said, slightly annoyed. "But what is her talent?"

"She can control the artefacts."

Scarlett? Scarlett!

"Is someone calling me?" I jump from the chair, looking around.

Scarlett!

"There, I've heard it again." I looked at Jubilee.

"I believe it's time for you to go home," she said. "Be careful who you trust in, and Scarlett, *please*, take care of Leah." Jubilee pleaded, pressing on the last words.

"I'll do what I can."

"I just pray it will be enough," she added concerned. "Leah, I know you can hear me. Do it the same. Imagine you push her, but this time backwards."

"Goodbye, Scarlett."

"See you soon, I guess."

I woke up being softly shaken by the shoulder.

"Scarlett? Scarlett, wake up!"

"What?" I answered irritated.

"Go home and sleep," Laura said to me, still keeping her hand on my shoulder. "You're exhausted! You've overworked yourself lately, always coming first and leaving last, at who knows what hour."

"I have a lot of things to do here," I said, half-asleep.

"Listen, I spoke with the Director, and he's more than happy to give you a few days off."

"But what about my work?" I waved around at all the stuff around my desk, raising my voice unintentionally. "If I'll take days off, I'll be off the schedule."

"No, you won't because you are ahead of it, anyway! Keep up like this, and you'll run out of thing to do." Laura crossed her arms. "Go home! Now!" She pointed the door.

I barely got up from the chair, but when I did, from my head and shoulders fell a black scarf. I looked at it confused as I didn't recognise it; it certainly wasn't mine. Perhaps Laura's, but then why was it on my head?

"Home! Now!"

"Fine, fine, I'm going. You don't have to be such a mom," I said, laughing while heading to the door. Stopping midway, I turned around on my heels and hugged Laura. "Thank you."

"Oh, my! You're welcome, sweets. By the way, what were you dreaming about? You were grumbling in your sleep.

Be careful who you trust in.

It certainly couldn't be about Laura, but maybe it wouldn't do any harm to be a bit more cautions.

"I dreamed of the time when I was a child and developed an interest in Greek mythology," I said.

"That must've been nice. Now I'm sorry I woke you up."

"Don't be. I prefer to dream in my bed, than on the top of the desk." I reached for the door handle.

"Scarlett, wait!" Laura jumped.

"Yes? I looked back, confused. Just a few minutes ago, she tried to kick me out the door, and now?

"If I were you, I would be more careful when and where I use my abilities. In my case, not everyone can see the energy waves, but you . . .," she hesitated.

"I what?" I asked, not liking the sound of it.

"You are a bit more obvious," Laura finally said.

Maybe it was just my fault, but I couldn't understand a thing she said.

"What you said right now makes absolutely no sense to me."

"Your hair, sweets, your hair. When you use your power, even if unconscious, it changes its colour, from black to red."

"Please tell me you're joking," I said, feeling the blood draining from my face, but her expression told me it was no joke. I untied my hair fast and pulled a strand in front of my eyes, but nothing looked different to me. I moved my eyes, questioning, to Laura, who watched me in silence.

"You can't see it now. Once you stop the energetic flow which nourishes and sustains your ability, everything returns to normal."

"Start what? Stop what? I don't know how this thing works; how it flows or however you called it, and I really have no desire to have my hair turning red around a bunch of people," I said helplessly, still holding the strand between my fingers.

"I will help you with that, but first, you need to get a better grasp of what you can do. Take advantage of these few days and explore your potential. Practice. Try to see how different emotions affect your ability and control over it. And most importantly, try to stay awake when you do this."

"But what about the changing hair? I don't think I can hide it if it happens in public."

Laura, with a solemn look on her face, raised her hand and stopped the avalanche of words which opened the path to a small panic attack.

"That's where I come in. You go home and leave it to me. Just because I had to discover my powers all by myself, it doesn't mean you have to do it as well. You are not alone. Go home, don't worry, and leave hiding your hair to me."

She winked and smiled, I waved and left.

I couldn't wait to get home, Laura's words reassured me to some extent, but now a strange curiosity made my soul burn. I had to test something, but first a final stop: ice-cream.

Chapter 7

Unbelievable.

The biggest ice-cream shop in the city and yet, my favourite favour just ran out. They had from the classic flavours like vanilla, chocolate, and fruits to the strangest combinations with garlic, sea-fruits, even a bacon limited edition. They had all that, except for what I wanted.

What did a girl have to do for a salted-caramel ice-cream?

I supposed my only option was to get something else and try to be happy about it. Ten minutes later and twenty different flavours in my basket, I went for the cashier.

If I wouldn't have been so absorbed by the inside of my bag while looking for my wallet, perhaps I would've noticed the person in front of me before stopping with my face in the middle of their back. I would have apologised, but I was too busy running after the ice cream cups that rolled between the other customers' feet. One, two, three . . . seventeen, eighteen, nineteen; one was missing.

"Did you lose something?" a male voice spoke from behind me.

Focusing on counting the cups, I failed to notice

him getting closer. It was the same person I'd bumped into and didn't apologise to, yet he returned my missing cup.

"Thank you, and I'm so sorry, I wasn't looking where I was going," I tried to explain.

"Don't worry about it, Scarlett. I think you're just tired," he smiled.

I gazed surprised at the man, who seemed in his late fifties and couldn't help but think how familiar he looked, but from where? And it wasn't just his appearance, but his voice as well. In fact, his voice seemed more familiar to me than the beard and grey hair, blue eyes, or the ancient framed glasses sitting on his nose. My brain tried hard to remember where I knew him from. It was evident that he knew me; he'd just called me by my name, but the answer came shortly.

"I take it that Laura passed the message."

Laura, how could I not have realised earlier? On the one hand, it was understandable since we rarely met, the conversations between us taking place on the phone and through emails. But what kind of an idiot doesn't remember their own boss's face?

"Yes, sir," I answered quickly. "Actually, I wanted to email you as soon as I got home. I would like to thank you for the time off and ask when you would like me to return to work."

"Worry not. In the short time since you joined the team, you've exceeded all my expectations. You earned yourself these few days, and before you ask; I will not deduct them from your annual leave, but I am going to pay them."

"That's very generous of you," I said, embarrassed. "You're too kind."

I didn't know what else I could say. I really wasn't expecting such a gesture from him. Behind that cold, rigid façade, was a big heart.

"Oh, child, this has nothing to do with generosity. I've lived a long life, and I've learned that it's good to show gratitude towards the people who work hard and from the heart. You are one of those people. A few days off are nothing compared with what you truly deserve."

I expected him to continue, but that never happened. The silence between us felt a little heavy, but I didn't dare to ask him what he meant. The situation became awkward, yet I didn't have a clue what I could possibly say. Slowly, my eyes slipped to his basket, which was empty.

"This is not good," he suddenly spoke, making me jump. "This is not good at all."

"I'm sorry, but what do you mean?" I frowned a bit.

"We stay here chatting while the ice-cream melts. Scarlett, go home, have a rest, and I'll see you at work on Tuesday morning."

Without waiting for an answer, he turned around and left, leaving the empty basket at the shop's entrance.

I got home faster than I thought, yet not fast

enough. The dark clouds gathered in the sky, hiding away the sun's light and warmth, making way to the cold raindrops. In mere minutes the small, rare drops turned into showers. The clouds became thicker, forbidding the light to pass through. Bolts of lightning whipped the tensed air, ripping frightened screams from children who were still outside. The wind shook everything; the shops' windows trembled, the cars' alarms went off, and people tried in vain to find shelter until the squall passed. It'd been a long time since I'd seen such a storm, and even longer since I'd been alone during one.

With water dripping from my hair and clothes, I threw the ice-creams in the freezer and running to the bedroom, I dumped my cold, wet outfit in the corner of the room. Before I managed to get my hands on a dry change of clothes, a clap of thunder shook the building from the ground, making my knees weak. I gave up entirely on the idea of dry clothes, and with seconds before another thunder brawled on the busy streets, I hid between the sheets and pulled the pillow over my head.

Focus, Scarlett, focus on something else. You are an adult woman, there is no reason to be afraid, I told myself.

Without taking my head out, I reached my hand, and after a few tries, I found the phone and the hands-free I'd left on the nightstand. With the music ringing in my ears, the pillow attenuating the storm's noises and the blanket warming my cold body, I was defeated by the exhaustion of the long and loaded days of work. I fell asleep, unintentionally.

I was already used to waking up in a different period, but this time, I arrived in a moment I would've wished to avoid.

I was in a dark place. The heavy curtains, covering the windows let only a few rays creep into the room. Seated on a chair by the bed, Leah fell asleep while watching her lady. Jubilee, once a dazzling beauty, now looked more dead than alive. She was so thin that it seemed as if even the sheet she was covered with could crush her at any moment under its insignificant weight, and her hair, once long, thick, and glossy, was now short and sparse.

"Scarlett?"

"I'm here, Leah. You can rest. I'll watch over Jubilee for you."

"Thank you."

That was the last thing she could say before falling back asleep. I could feel how worn out she really was. Physically, she wasn't too bad, but psychically, she was drained. And all I could do to help was to let her rest.

I fixed my eyes on the figure sleeping on the bed.

Her chest movement assured me she was still alive, but they were so heavy and rare that it was hard to tell how long she could keep on. From time to time, a whimper broke through the dry lips, as if she was in pain. I wished I could do something to alleviate her suffering, but it was beyond my capabilities.

Sitting on the edge of the bed, so I could be closer if she needed me, I gently squeezed her cold hand when she cried again. I wanted to reassure her that she wasn't alone, but then Jubilee opened her eyes and looked at me.

"Where's Leah?" she asked, her voice weak and broken.

"She's sleeping," I told her, whispering. "Do you want me to wake her up?"

"No."

"Is there anything you need?" I asked, worried.

"I need you to listen carefully. Take Leah as far away from this place as possible."

"She won't want to leave."

"I'll tell her myself. If she stays, she will suffer a lot and only because of me."

I could feel the remorse in her voice, but I didn't understand. Leah loved this place and the people in it. It was normal for her to suffer once Jubilee was gone, after all, she was the person she held most dearly.

"Why would it be your fault?" I tried to sound comforting. "You can't control what's happening to you, and Leah understands that. She suffers but understands."

"You are the one who doesn't understand," she protested. "I am the one who told my father years ago that in our house would come a young girl with the ability to control the artefacts. That was the moment the future changed irreversibly." But a violent cough interrupted her protest. She covered her mouth with the white night gown's sleeve she wore, but when she removed it, it was full of blood.

After she calmed down a bit, Jubilee continued.

"I'm begging you, save Leah of what's to come. Take her away from here; as far as possible, where my father won't be able to find her. Please, Scarlett."

Talking was a considerable effort for her, quickening her breathing.

"But how can I do that? I don't know anything about this place, and not to mention, I can't be with her all the time.

"She's strong. She'll be fine. Search in the jewellery box," she struggled to point, with a trembling hand, to a box in front of the mirror. "You'll find a recommendation letter, which will help her find work no matter where she'll go, and, also, take the black-stones necklace. If she is ever in trouble, she'll be able to sell that without too many questions."

I got up and went to the box. I found the letter on the very bottom and the necklace in a small black pouch. Taking them both, I shoved them in a pocket. When I returned by the bed, Jubilee had her eyes closed and was breathing with much more effort than before.

"Scarlet . . . call Leah," she barely said.

"No, no, no," I panicked, understanding exactly what she meant. "You can't do that. *Leah, you need to wake up!* You can't give up now. Just a little bit longer. *LEAH!*

I felt suddenly pulled back in the spectator's seat, and Leah's desperate voice cried through the room.

"My Lady!" she fell on her knees, by the bed.

"Leah, sweet child. You need to leave this house, and so do I, we'll just go in different ways." Jubilee patted her head.

"My Lady, please don't talk this way." Leah pleaded.

"This is for the best. My time is almost up. Leave, and don't look back. You can't stay here any longer."

"But this place is my home, please don't chase me away, not now," she answered amid tears, taking Jubilee's hand.

"Leah, I'm not chasing you away, but if you stay, nothing good will come. It's time we both moved on. Go . . . and may the gods keep you safe."

Leah tried hard to stop crying, listening quietly to her Lady's words.

"Leave my friend, my sister . . . my child."

When the last words left her lips, the last breath left her body, leaving behind a broken-hearted child, who once again lost her home and family. With her head on the edge of the bed and still holding Jubilee's hand, Leah sobbed.

"Leah, I'm sorry."

I didn't get any answer from her.

"I know it's painful, but we need to leave."

No movement, no sound except the sighs that had become more regular. If I hadn't participated at this scene from the backstage, maybe I would've never really comprehended what she was going through. I wouldn't have felt the wound which consumed her soul and burned her heart.

Leah was unable to leave Jubilee's inert body, and I couldn't blame her.

"Leah, let me take over. You don't have to do a thing," I tried to convince her.

I felt a short hesitation from her, but then the fabric of the sheets was under the palm of my hand. Standing up fast, I wiped the tears off of my face. Lady Jubilee said to leave as fast and as far as possible. With the letter and the necklace already in one of the dress's pockets, I entered the side room, which belonged to Leah. I couldn't take too many things. This had to be a light, fast trip. In a bag, I packed a dress and undergarments. From the untouched food tray, I took the bread, the cheese, and the fruits, and without looking back, I went out the door and down the long manor's corridor.

I knew where I had to go; to the back of the house. But I've been there only once before and could only vaguely remember the way. Leah wasn't much help in the state she was in, sinking in so deep that I almost couldn't feel her anymore. It was as if she'd built a wall between us, but with all this, she'd walked by there so many times that her body knew automatically where to turn and what doors to open. It was a real miracle that we didn't meet anyone inside the house, but the danger was far from over. Now we just had to cross the back yard, without being noticed. I ran as fast as I could to the shelter provided by the trees where we were safe.

Maybe the gods really were on our side.

Chapter 8

"All these books are useless!" he shouted, frustrated, smashing his fists against the massive desk, grinding his teeth. "I need to find that girl! I need to find that blasted Watch."

In one move, he threw everything he had on the desk to the floor, howling in anger like a caged, wild beast. It made no difference to him that all those books, letters, and diagrams were left as a legacy from one generation to another, dating back hundreds of years ago.

He was running out of time.

"Cursed Watch!" he swore under his breath.

According to all the research made along the years, only one conclusion was reached. The Watch revealed its location only to certain people; people with particular abilities.

Jubilee knew where it was, and also knew who the girl that could control it was, but she stubbornly refused to tell him.

The thought that his own daughter hindered his research drove him mad more than the fact that he had a hard time decrypting the three diagrams which could at least give him a clue regarding the location, if not pointing it out precisely.

It was well known it should be somewhere inside the house, but in time, a lot of changes had been made. He personally checked every room, every corner, the greenhouse, the cellar, the attic, even the stables, and the servants' rooms, without avail.

Straightening his back and arranging his coat, he went to the window. In his mind, there were only two options left: he could either find the Watch, or give up. But if he gave up, all the efforts and sacrifices until then would've been useless. All those moments when his beloved wife needed him, and he wasn't there . . . and now, in any moment, their daughter was going to follow her mother's steps, and he would be all alone.

His lips stretched in a cold smile, and his eyes burned impatiently. Once Jubilee has gone to waste, there would be nothing left in his path. He was going to rummage the entire domain if needed.

Hysterical laughter began to shake his whole body and clenching his fist, he punched it through the window's glass. Glass shards of all shapes fell off the broken window, along with the red splashes of blood that trickled from his arm.

I will get that Watch even if I have to step on bodies, he thought, holding his hurt arm.

A gentle knock on the door interrupted his thoughts, and Emma came in the room with a sombre look on her face.

"I apologise for bothering you, My Lord. It's about Lady Jube–"

"Make the necessary preparations," he cut her

short, without looking back from the window. He didn't need to hear the rest as he knew exactly what it was all about.

"Yes, My Lord." Emma left the room, but not before she glanced at the broken window and the shards at the Earl's feet.

He was going to get his hands on that Watch, but first, he had a funeral to attend.

Chapter 9

The path I walked on bent through the trees, leading deeper and deeper, as if towards the heart of the forest. It was wide enough for a small carriage but didn't seem used too often. I kept walking, not knowing which way I was going. Maybe if Leah were here with me, she would've known where we headed, but I couldn't reach her no matter what I said. I started to feel a bit lonely, but I made my decision to stay by her side for as long as I could.

I went on, but the day wasn't going to last endlessly. I should find shelter for the night, but where? We were in the middle of the forest. After a few more hours, in a meadow, I discovered a little wooden hut. I couldn't believe it was anything else but blind luck, but what did I know? I knocked on the door, yet it looked like no one was home. I pushed it a bit, but without any resistance, the door opened, revealing its dusty interior.

"Hello? Anyone home?" I shouted, opening the door completely.

I didn't take any steps inward. What if someone actually lived there? Maybe they were just gone for a walk or something similar.

"It's fine, Scarlett, you can go in. no one lives here."

Leah's voice startled me. I'd gotten so comfortable in her body that it almost slipped my mind that it wasn't truly mine.

"The place belongs to the Conwells," Leah went on with her explanation. *"This is where Lady Jubilee came, when she wanted to get away from home, have some quiet, or write. This place was her refuge, and since it's still on the family's land, it didn't raise a problem."*

"But why would it be a problem?" I asked, refraining myself from asking how she felt.

"Her health being rather poor, and getting worse from day to day, made it difficult for her to travel long distances. As a solution, the Earl built this place, close to the main house, yet far enough."

"What do you mean close to the house? We've constantly been going for a few hours!"

"If you take the path, then yes, it would take a few hours, but there is a shortcut known by few which will cut the time in half."

"And you left me to walk all that time without saying a word," I sighed, tired and crushed on a chair. I couldn't really get mad at her. *"It's quite small, and simple,"* I added.

"It was built after the lady's precise indications. The Earl wanted to make it bigger, with separate bedrooms, a living room, and kitchen, but My Lady was against it."

I looked around in amazement. There was a single, big room, with two beds in one corner, a shelf with a few books, a table with two chairs and a hob where food could be prepared. Simple, without any decorations, with nothing to reveal when it was built or to whom it belonged to. Just a hut in the woods.

Fascinated by the place I was in; I couldn't tell what was happening in Leah's heart until I felt tears streaming down my cheeks. That place, to the smallest detail, reminded her of Jubilee. We couldn't stay there.

"Leah," I said, "there's no need for us to stay here. If you want, we can keep moving. I'm sure we'll be able to find shelter someplace else."

"Thank you, but it's alright. I'll be fine; besides, you need rest."

"If you say so . . . but I'll need your help with something."

"With what?" she asked, curious.

"Do you think you can light up the fire and the lamp? I haven't got a clue how to do it," I told her, a bit embarrassed.

"You don't know how to light up an oil lamp?" she responded stunned. *"Then how do you illuminate your house?"*

"We have electricity."

"Electricity? What is that?" She became interested.

"Lightning, for example."

"You mean there are bolts of lightning in your houses?" she asked, puzzled.

"No, no, no; it's a bit more complicated than that. It all started from a bolt of lightning, and in time, humans learned, or I should probably say they will learn, to

create electric power out of different sources: like from the sun's power, wind, and even from the speed with which the water flows. There will be devices which will take all that and turn it into electricity which will then be sent to homes around the world through cables."

"I'd wish to see your world. Tell me more about this electricity, please."

I tried my best to define electricity and electric systems while she effortlessly lit the fire. I'm not sure how much she understood since I couldn't say I knew too much, either. As a permanent part of my daily life, I never really thought what it is and where it comes from, but I think I made clear enough that oil lamps no longer belonged in a modern house, their place being only in museums.

After she fixed the light and heat, Leah hid again, letting me lead. I pulled out the food, and placing it on the table, I ate slowly when I heard Leah again.

"On this table, Lady Jubilee taught me how to read and write. She had so much patience with me." I listened in silence, not knowing what to say. *"She even made a special book for me, so I could learn easier. It should be on the shelf behind you, next to the other books."*

I stood up from the table and turned towards the small bookshelf. I found, indeed, something that looked like a spelling book, but it looked a bit more complex. Besides letters and general spelling and writing rules, there were also some mathematical equations of reduced difficulty. Perhaps something similar to what I'd learned in the first two or three years of school.

"I'd wish if I ever have children, to teach them how to read and write after this book." I felt a bittersweet smile coming from her, but then quiet.

Once I finished eating, I packed the rest and put them back in the bag, after all, tomorrow was another day. I moved the lamp on the small table by the beds, and though didn't find it very tempting to turn it off and be left in the dark, I just turned it down a bit. I laid on one of the beds, listening. I was afraid to fall asleep, risking waking up in my own bed. I couldn't leave Leah alone, so I decided the best course would be to remain awake for as long as I could.

I had no means to tell how much time had passed or how long until morning, which turned out to be somewhat maddening. The noises of the night were fascinating, and at the same time, sinister. I'd spent nights in nature before, this wasn't the first time. Both in college, and university I used to go camping quite often with friends, family . . . with Jared. Strange how only now I recalled him. Crossing my arms under my head, I watched the small flame's light dancing on the hut's wooden ceiling, while in a tree nearby an owl called her sisters.

My brain was so bored it started fluttering through memories, some pleasant, while others were utterly useless. I was time to put it to work; if I left it in this state of uncensored freedom, who knew what dark corners would stir next. It was enough Leah was depressed, there was no point for me to slip down the same slope.

The first thing I had to do was to figure out where we were, as then to figure out where we were heading, but how could I do that without Leah? How nice would've been a GPS now, or at least a map, though a map without a satellite localisation option wasn't too useful.

Hold it! GPS? Satellite? Seriously, Scarlett? You are two hundred years in the past. Focus.

There was no point. I gave up fretting, it was best to wait for the morning and hope Leah would be in a bit more of a sociable state. Getting out of bed, I stopped by the window through which the light of the full moon cascaded. From my time, from the bustling city, I could rarely see such a pure moon, and the stars around it were an even rarer occurrence. I stayed there, leaning against the hard, wooden wall, watching outside as the light that flowed from the sky caressed every strand of grass and played with the insects' wings and the birds' feathers, making them glow, as if from within.

With this image in front of my eyes, as if from a fairy-tale, intertwined with the night's vivid song, I was no longer afraid. Somehow, I had the feeling that everything would turn out alright; somehow, I felt at peace.

The wind made the leaves rustle, and sometimes a twig to crack. The bird's cries through the night seemed a melody meant to attract prey straight in their sharp claws, and from time to time a wings' flutter distracted me, flying over the hut, disappearing between the trees, leaving behind only the steps which grew steadily closer to the cabin.

Steps?

With a bang, the door flew open, hitting the wall, and two men entered the once spacious room. Tall, unkempt for some time, and smelling of alcohol and sweat, they moved forward toward me. The dim light in the room made them seem creepier than they might've genuinely been, the shadows emphasising their carved by life features. Perhaps, if I were in my body, I wouldn't have felt intimidated, but Leah seemed to be shorter than me, and by comparison, the two men looked like mountains. Their vicious smiles told me they meant anything but good news, and without saying a word, one of them dashed at me, while the other remained propped up near the door which now hung only by one hinge.

With an arm outstretched to grab me, he did not expect at any moment of resistance. I caught him with both hands by the wrist and twisting around, I threw him over my shoulder. A stifled sound was heard when he hit the floor and lost consciousness. Leah might've been small-sized, but all the work at the manor made her rather strong. The second man looked at his friend in disbelief, and with his face writhing in anger, he spat between his clenched teeth.

"You little whore!"

He rushed to me with the apparent intention of hitting, but, unlucky for him, he seemed more affected by the alcohol's haze than his friend. Being slightly unsteady on his feet, it only took a step to the side and a forceful shove in the back to send him with his head straight into the wall, then dropping to the floor, still.

Even with my breath strained from the effort, I felt grateful for the long-ago martial arts' classes my mom made me take as a child, for years in a row. Even so, I didn't want to repeat the experience too soon.

There wasn't enough time to catch my breath. We had to leave, once again on the run. I hurriedly grabbed the bag and put out the lamp, but before I could get out the door in the chilly night air, a third man appeared on the threshold.

This one seemed different from the other two, with a thin body, contoured by the moonlight and an elegant posture. He didn't seem to be a danger, but I wasn't going to try my luck. Hastily, I attempted to hit him, but he grabbed my arm effortlessly.

Beginner's luck, I said to myself.

I tried again, with my free hand, yet not for long. Like reading my thoughts, he caught my other arm and pushing me gently against a wall, he detained both my arms over my head. He shouldn't have been a challenge comparing to the other two, but appearances can be deceiving. The place where his hand held mine began to burn, and my palms to sweat. The few rays of light, entering the hut through the windows and the broken door, were far from enough to see the stranger in front of me, but I didn't need any light to feel his body's warmth, barely a few inches away. I wanted so badly to hit with my knee between his legs that it was almost painful, but the never-ending fabric layers from my dress hindered such free moves.

Expertly, he wrapped, almost imperceptibly, something around my wrists and then turning his eyes towards the two unconscious men on the floor, he sighed deeply.

"A real waste of money. I wasn't expecting them to be so easily defeated, at least not by a young woman such as yourself, Leah, or perhaps I should call you Scarlett?"

His warm voice took me by surprise, but at the hearing of my name I wanted to take a step back, to move away from the man in front of me, but I was stuck between the wall and his unmoving body.

"Who are you?" I asked between my gritted teeth, swallowing dryly. "What do you want?"

"I'm here to take Leah home."

"How do you know about me?" I asked, trying to overcome my frustration that I couldn't get away from his grasp, although he only used one hand.

"How?" he answered, amused. "From Lady Jubilee, of course. After all, she was the only one who knew, but it seems she didn't tell you about me."

"Well, I'm sorry to disappoint you, but during our short meetings, we had better subjects to discuss than boys. And if you truly know from Jubilee, then you should be aware that she asked me to take Leah as far away as possible from here. To leave without looking back and never return no matter what."

"And she told me, as clearly as possible, to do all in my power to protect her, but I can't do this from a distance."

Neither of us realised we'd raised our voices until one of the men on the floor began to wail. He stepped away from me, leaving me to crave his warmth when the cold air took his place, and with a single blow, he brought the man back to unconsciousness. This was my chance to run away, or it would've been if he wouldn't have tied my hands by a ridiculously resilient hook. I pulled with all my strength, but it didn't even move. Biting my inner cheek, I clenched my fists. I'm not violent by nature, but I really wanted to hit something right about now.

"*Scarlett . . . please, I want to go home,*" her voice was empty, without strength.

"*But what about what Jubilee said? She told you to run far away, or else you'll be in great danger.*" I tried to persuade her.

"*Please, take me home. I trust him.*"

"*Well, I don't.*"

"*You will.*"

"*I wouldn't be so sure.*"

"*I'm begging you, Scarlett, just take me home. Tell Chance I'm ready to return to the manor.*"

My eyes ran to the shadow, which moved agilely in the dark. I opened my mouth to call him, but a realisation hit me. Leah begged *me* to take her home when she could've just taken her body back and gone by herself. It was a simple answer to that. She wanted to stay hidden for a little while longer, which is why she needed me.

Oh, Leah . . .

"Ready to go, My Lady?" his voice came from somewhere nearby.

"Yes, I'm ready," I sighed.

"Hmm . . . I didn't expect you to give up so fast. What are you scheming?" he strode lightly, getting closer.

"Don't be delusional, I haven't given up." I frowned at him uselessly since he couldn't see me. "But Leah did, and she wants to go home. This is her body and her life, so in the end, the decision is hers entirely."

"I see."

He sounded disappointed as he reached and un-did the binding on my wrists. My arms fell, slightly numb on the sides of my body because of the posi-tion in which they've been tied, and flexing my fists a few times, I tried to get rid of the tingling feeling from under my skin. Chance waited for me uncom-plainingly, and when I was ready, he led me to the hut's door.

As soon as we stepped out, the moon lit us both, and the face of the man, hitherto hidden in the dark-ness, was revealed to me. The light wasn't strong enough to distinguish the colour of his hair or outfit, but it was enough to see his fine features and elegant clothes, possibly custom made. As far as I could tell, Chance probably belonged to a family with a pretty good status, but in that case, why would he bother to such extent for a servant girl? Sure, Jubilee might've asked him, but that didn't change the rank difference among the two of them.

Who are you, Chance? Who are you that Leah trusts you so much?

We walked a little on the dark path, until, not too far from the hut, tied to a branch was a black horse. If he didn't fret at the sight of his owner, maybe I wouldn't have noticed him.

Stopping in my way, I looked confused at the big animal in front of me.

"Please tell me you don't want to go back horse-back riding," I said, seriously concerned.

"You haven't ridden a horse before?" he snorted amused, caressing the horse's thick mane. "Then how do you go around?"

"We have other ways; faster and safer ways."

"There's nothing to be afraid of. Come."

He reached his arm for me, but I wasn't convinced it was a good idea to get closer. Taking my hand, he pulled me closer, and pressing his chest against my back, he resumed stroking the horse as earlier, with his hand over mine.

"See, he won't hurt you."

The mane felt soft and glossy under my palm, and the short snorts made it clear that he loved the attention he received. I liked it, too. It was the first time in my life I got to be so close to a horse, not to mention patting him, but what I enjoyed the most was the warmth felt on my back and the gentle way he guided my hand.

"Moonlight, tonight we have a complete novice with us, so you'll need to be on your best behaviour."

As if understanding, he neighed wiggling his head.

"You named your horse Moonlight?"

Without answering, Chance placed his hands on my waist, and with ease, lifted me onto the saddle.

"I'm going to fall!" I screamed, grabbing the edge of the saddle tightly. "Get me down, I'll fall."

"You won't fall," he said, smiling. Climbing behind me and grabbing the reins, he framed me between his arms, supporting me. "If you are so tense it won't be too pleasant for you. Try to relax a little."

"I don't think I can," I replied, terrified.

He wrapped an arm around my waist and pulled me closer, once again placing my back to his broad chest, and with his smooth, smoky voice, he whispered in my ear. "I'm here, beside you. I won't let you fall."

I only said, "Thank you." What else was there to say? I was literally in his hands. If he hadn't liked something, it wouldn't have been hard for him to push me off of the horse, but my instinct told me he'd never do something like that. He was a perfect gentleman. Apart from the moment when he sent two brutes after me and tied me to a hook, he acted relatively nicely. I shook my head, dismissing the thought. But I still wanted to hit him; only once, hard.

I chased away all the negative thoughts from my mind and tried to enjoy the ride. It was quite relaxing; the hooves' rhythmic sound, the wind, the crickets' song, the fireflies floating between the trees, Chance's voice . . .

"How many times have you travelled here so far?"

"This would be the third time, I think," I answered, jumping a little in surprise.

Feeling my reaction, he pulled me even closer, and laughing, he continued.

"So, Jubilee was right after all . . ."

"What do you mean?" I asked, confused.

"She told me I would meet, through Leah, a young woman; very different from all the others. When she first told me, I didn't understand much, but then she clarified. I was well aware of her talent, but even so, it found it hard to believe. That was at least until Leah ran away; or rather, *you* did."

"Speaking of running away; do you think she'll be in trouble? This Earl of yours, what kind of person is he? Do you think he will forgive her?"

"I don't know. Up until now, Lord Conwell was that person who helped everyone without expecting anything in return, warm, and understanding. But Jubilee warned me that with her death, that man would disappear. So, I don't know what's going to happen from here on."

"Leah, maybe you want to reconsider returning to the manor. Leah?"

Utter silence. I put my hand on my chest and

closing my eyes, I tried to find her, to feel her, and I did. Hiding deeply, still sighing from time to time, she'd fallen asleep.

"How's Leah?" he asked, concerned.

"She's sleeping."

"Good. She'll need plenty of rest for what's to come."

"Meaning?"

"There's a lot of work at the manor, and now with Lady Jubilee gone, a lot of things need to be prepared for the funeral and mourning."

I frowned at his answer. All he said was true, indeed, buy why did it feel as if there was more than that?

Chapter 10

Chance kept Moonlight to a languid pace, and he didn't seem to like it at all; snorting and neighing every time Chance tempered his pace. He was going so slow that I could've kept up with him on foot, but he probably did it, so I wouldn't get scared. I began to feel comfortable on the saddle, but I don't think I would've had the courage to ride by myself.

By the time we got back to the manor, it had already dawned.

In front of the back door, the same one we'd left through, a woman in a black dress with a grim expression on her face was waiting for us. I recognised her as Emma, the woman who was made responsible for Leah after her parents left her here.

Chance stopped the horse near her and helped me get off, but as soon as my feet touched the ground, I woke up with a heavy palm across my face.

"You stupid child!" she barked at me. "How dare you show such disrespect to this family?"

"Stop it, Emma!" Chance demanded, stretching an arm between the revolted woman and me.

Puffing her chest out and pressing her lips together tightly, she turned on her heels and stomped off back into the house.

I covered my burning cheek with a hand, and looking at Chance, who still had his arm protectively in front of me, and his eyes fixed on Emma's back, I whispered, "Thank you."

"Anything for you, My Lady," he said with half a smile. "Now try to wake up Leah; I'm rather sure the Earl will want to see her."

"Let me try. *Leah?*"

Nothing.

"Leah, we are back at the manor."

Quiet.

"You can't hide forever. It's time for me to go home."

"Please don't!" she pleaded. *"Please stay a bit longer. Don't leave me alone; not now."*

"Leah, I can't meet the Earl."

"Neither can I . . ."

"I think we have a problem," I told Chance, biting my lip.

"What happened?" he frowned.

"She won't come out." I turned livid. "She doesn't want to meet the Earl."

"Then this doesn't give us any other option. You will have to replace her."

"Me?" I shouted. "Are you out of your mind? I can't do that. I don't know how I'm supposed to act, and the last thing I want is to cause Leah even more trouble."

"Shut up and listen to me." he grabbed my shoulders, forcing me to look into his amber eyes. "All you have to do is to keep your eyes on the floor and don't raise them for anything in the world. Understood?" he tried to ease my tension.

"But what if he asks me something, and I have to answer?" I asked agitated. "I know nothing about this place or about the people here . . . nothing." I felt hopeless.

"Calm down and leave the talking to me. You just focus on a spot on the floor."

My heart climbed into the middle of my throat as I came face to face with the doors behind which the Earl was expecting Leah.

"Everything will be fine; just remember what you must do and leave the rest to me," Chance tried to encourage me.

Without waiting for any sort of confirmation from me, he knocked on the door and went in, with me following closely.

"Never. Never in my life have I've been disrespected to such extent."

I was tempted to raise my eyes, hearing the cold, gruff voice coming from somewhere from my right, but I didn't. The Earl came near me, and even with my head bent, I could see him up to his chest. He seemed quite tall; dressed in black from head to toe; the exception being a white shirt. He held a cane in his hand, for the sake of fashion as he did not seem to need it to move around.

"You need to learn respect, and I will teach it to you myself."

It didn't take me long to understand what he meant as he raised his cane. I closed my eyes and tightened my body. I heard the sound of the strike but didn't feel a thing. Opening my eyes, I saw the cane a few fingers away from my abdomen; in Chance's hand.

"What's the meaning of this, Colton?" the Earl thundered.

"Forgive me, My Lord, but the story is much more complicated than it might seem at first. Contrary to what might have reached your ears, that Leah ran away, the truth is that she was kidnapped."

Seriously?

"I managed to catch them just in time. Otherwise, who knows to what horrors the poor girl would have been subjected to."

"Kidnapped you say? By whom?" the Earl asked unconvinced.

"Two men with a history of such behaviour. They used to capture young girls and sell them to pleasure houses." Chance kept his stance.

"Is that so? And where would those two be as we speak?"

"Properly tied in the wooden hut, and if I may, I would like as soon as we finish here to personally hand them over to the Scotland Yard detectives."

"Impressive, but I can't say I expected any less from you. I wasn't wrong when I offered you the job; you are genuinely a promising young man.

"Thank you, My Lord." Chance bowed his head, and we left the room, closing the doors behind us.

That was more stressful than expected. I opened my mouth, but Chance got ahead of me.

"We can't talk here. Follow me," he whispered.

I followed him, more running than walking, trying not to fall behind until we reached a side room.

"As I said, everything turned out alright," he said, shutting the door, but not before he checked if we'd been seen.

"Fine?" I shouted at him. "Are you joking right now? What about your hand?"

He must've expected me to be forever grateful because my backlash caught him off-guard.

"It's nothing."

He tried to hide the hurt palm, but I was faster. I seized his sleeve and lifted his hand. With gentle touches, I felt the affected area, which had begun to swell.

"It's not—"

"Don't talk!"

I kept palpating his hand until I was satisfied. I looked him in the eye, touching the red-hot area again; no reaction; no twitch, no jolt, but it was impossible for him to not feel anything.

"Nothing feels broken, but I recommend you put something cold on it."

"Are you worried about me?" he asked, pleased.

"Certainly not!" I said, still holding his hand in mine, "But, that hit you took was meant for me, so. . ." I bit my lower lip, averting my eyes.

"Don't think about it." He raised my face. "I did only what any gentleman would've done. A woman shouldn't be touched not even with a flower; let alone a cane."

"Said the one who sent two hoodlums after me and tied me to a hook," I raised an eyebrow, and a playful smile bloomed on my lips.

"As it's said, everything is permitted in love and war."

"Are we at war?" I slightly tilted my head innocently.

"Not at all." Chance showed a smug smile.

"Speaking of those two . . . did you plan this kidnapping story from the beginning?"

"Yes, but there was an unpredicted element."

"What?"

"You, overpowering those two. I was supposed to do that, that way, winning your trust."

"So, you wanted to be the knight in shining armour, but ended up being the villain."

"Am I still the villain?" he asked slightly concerned.

With a finger, I tapped my chin, weighing all the facts. "Well . . . Leah trusts you, you defended me in front of Emma and took a blow for me, so I presume that kind of saves you."

"There is one more thing I need to do." With a step back and a deep bow, he continued, reaching his hand for mine. "Chance Colton, Lord Conwell's Secretary, at your service, My Lady."

Playing his game, I offered him my hand, and with a clumsy reverence, I introduced myself.

"Scarlett Aubyn, a nosey woman from the future. It's a genuine pleasure, good Sir."

He turned my hand, and softly kissed the interior of my wrist, making my blood pressure rise, and looking deep into my eyes, he pushed a rebel strand of hair behind my ear, caressing my cheek with the tip of his finger when he pulled back his hand.

"Aubyn? The Aubyn's domain is at a short distance from here. Perhaps you are their descendant?"

"I couldn't tell," I said, trying to focus back on our conversation. "I'm not even too sure where I am at the moment."

With a hand on the middle of my back, Chance led me to a window from where I could see the main road.

"If you follow that road," he showed me, "you'll reach London in about an hour."

"London–"

My words got interrupted by a strong wave of dizziness, and a mist settled over my eyes. Supporting my waist, Chance sat me down on one of the chairs nearby.

"Scarlett!" Leah's voice echoed in my mind.

"Leah, what's happening?" My eyelids were getting heavier, and I could hardly keep my eyes open.

"Forgive me, this is all my fault," she said remorsefully. *"You're exhausted. You need to rest."*

"But what about you? Will you be alright?" I was falling asleep.

"You don't need to worry about me anymore. I'll be fine now. I'm not alone. Thank you, dear friend."

"Goodbye, My Lady," Chance said softly, kissing my hand again. "We shall meet again soon."

Soon. . .

Chapter 11

I woke up to Bon Jovi rocking "Living on a Prayer" in my ears. I was back in my comfortable bed, with the pillow over my head. The storm I'd hid from was now just light rain. Glancing at my phone, I was surprised to see it had only been a little over three hours since I fell asleep. Three hours here and almost twenty-four on the other side. I didn't want to leave my bed; I wanted to go back.

Turning from one side to another in the big bed, I got tangled in my own hair, which still had some rosy tints. I recalled Laura's advice; I had to experiment. Jumping from the bed, I headed for the bathroom's mirror. Who cared about clothes anymore? Since there was no one else in the house, I might as well spend the day naked.

In the few seconds it took me to get to the mirror, my hair turned black completely. I tried to concentrate, to make it red again, but it didn't work. I tried to think of the past, of its architecture, music, atmosphere, and of Leah, but that didn't work, either. Putting my hand on my chest, I felt my heartbeat. Maybe instead of thinking about Leah as a person, I should think about the sensation I had when we were together; when the connection between us was at its peak, and I could sense all her fears and feelings.

"Leah?" I tried calling her name, but when I got no answer in return, I began to feel ridiculous, like I was summoning spirits.

Leaning over the sink, I pressed my forehead against the cold mirror and sighed from the bottom of my heart.

Maybe I really should get some rest before trying again.

A ruby glitter slipped through the front of my eyes when a strand of hair slid off my shoulder, and a heartfelt sensation blossomed in my chest. Stepping back from the mirror, my eyes widened. Hair by hair, my thick straight locks, turned from black to scarlet.

"Leah!" I called her again.

"Hello, Scarlett. I missed you."

Her voice was calm and livelier. I could feel her smiling. I fought the impulse of closing my eyes; I had to do this awake and learn how to control it.

"How long has it been?"

"Almost two months."

"Two months!"

But that's ridiculous; I returned less than half an hour ago.

"Is something wrong?" Leah asked.

"Um? No, sorry, I was just thinking about something. Leah, can you see what I see right now?"

"No, I can only hear your voice, but it feels different from before; as if you are somewhere far away."

"I see. So, I am the only one who can cross back and forth."

I looked at my mirrored image and at my red hair, reaching down to my hips; incontestable confirmation of my abilities, of my talent. A proof which I needed away from people's eyes.

"Leah?"

"Yes, Scarlett?"

"Are you alright?"

"I'm fine; we all are. We knew we were going to lose Lady Jubilee sooner or later and that somehow helped us get over it a bit easier, but . . ."

"But . . .?"

"It's the Earl, h-he acts differently. He often locks himself in his study for days in a row, and when he finally comes out, he's always scowling at everyone around him, and he became violent. Before he didn't believe in corporal punishments, but now he's applying them himself."

"But that's terrible! Why would he do that?"

"I don't know."

"Leah, you need to get out of there. I think this is what Jubilee was talking about when she told you to leave."

"But I can't do that. I'm the one who chose this life the moment I returned. No matter what, I can't leave."

"I'm sorry I can't be there for you."

"Don't worry about it. Even if you're not here, I can always count on Chance."

"I hope you're right."

The connection broke imperceptibly, my hair suddenly changing colour.

I was relieved knowing that Leah was better, but the count's behavioural changes were worrying. And there was also Chance. . .

I hope his hand is alright.

And not only that. Leah, the one that first appeared in my dreams; the one who made me believe and asked for my help; I still didn't know what she wanted from me, and I wasn't too sure how to find out.

That's it; I had to get back to bed.

I didn't take more than two steps before I heard the noisy protests of my neglected stomach. Maybe it would be a good idea to eat something first.

The night seemed too short, and although I hadn't woken up earlier than lunchtime, I still felt tired. Two hours later, I had sunk again in the comfort of my pillows and didn't wake up until the following morning.

Chapter 12

It was nice to have some time for myself, but also unbelievably dull. As weird as it may sound, I didn't want to be there, but in the past, with Leah.

Reluctantly, I turned on the TV and started changing channels without being particularly attracted to anything. The irony made me stop at a historical movie: *Emma–a Victorian romance*. A love story between a maid and a young man with a good status, in a period full of social restrictions. A taboo tale, which after my opinion should've been called a drama rather a romance. I'd seen the movie before, so I knew how it ended. The two lovers are getting separated by the times' rigidity, by family and all those around them. He ends up marrying for status and fortune, and Emma gets to a house where she's physically and mentally abused until the end of her life. Somehow this whole story made me think of Leah and her situation. Maybe there wasn't a rich, handsome heir in the picture, but the Earl's behaviour and Jubilee's warnings didn't give me peace.

By her words, the Earl would try to break the seals and use the Watch's powers, but she overlooked telling me how he would do it; and especially what I could do about it. The most logical answer would be for me to stop him. But how? First, I didn't even know where the clock was, and then I was dependent on Leah and her body.

I let my head fall on the back of the couch while listening to the movie's soundtrack.

"Leah, what do you want from me? What do you want me to do?" I asked out loud, not expecting an answer.

I had to figure out what I had to do next; how I could help her. I lacked pieces of information, but I had to work with what I had. Apparently, I couldn't get to Leah anytime I wanted, which made my ability untrustworthy. Also, to be able to get in her time, I had to have my eyes closed and implicitly fall asleep, which could not happen in public places or at work. Not to mention the changing hair.

I closed my eyes and tried to breathe slowly; in through the nose, out through the mouth, in through the nose, out through the mouth. Although this was an exercise meant to calm my mind, it did nothing more than increase the level of agitation I felt, causing me to burst out.

"How the hell can I do something if I don't know what I'm supposed to do?" I shouted, punching the couch, except that my fists did not touch the soft pillows. There was no need to open my eyes to grasp that I was no longer on the living room's couch.

I knew where I was.

"You'll make wrinkles before time if you keep frowning like that."

"I suppose you don't have those kind of worries," I said sarcastically.

I looked at Leah, who was floating among the stars beside me. She had a playful smile, but her eyes were just as sad. Without wanting to, I noticed that her dress was different; now it was coffee-coloured and much simpler and more conservative than the one before, and the hair was tied in a back knot, making her look much older.

"How do you do that?" I asked.

"Do what?" she answered puzzled.

"Your dress is different, and so is your hair."

"Easy . . ." She smiled.

Without adding anything else, she snapped her fingers, and the whole look changed instantly. Her dress was now blue with low shoulders, and the hair was arranged at the top of the head in a sophisticated style.

"Hmm, or maybe something a bit more modern would be better," she said to herself.

She snapped her fingers again and this time changed into a pair of flared trousers and a greenish blouse, with her hair undone and wearing a bandana on her head. The style was more from the '70s and '80s, but considering the period she came from, I think it could be called modern.

"Oh, wow! Leah, that's amazing!" I clapped my hands.

"Wait, that's not all. I can even change your clothes and the scenery," she continued, thrilled.

"Really?" I was amazed.

With another snap of her fingers, I woke up dressed in a ball gown, seafoam-coloured, with crinoline and a tight corset around the ribs, which barely allowed me to breathe.

"This is not very comfortable," I said.

In a split second, the tightness from around my waist and chest disappeared, letting me breathe with ease. Relieved that I could breathe again, I didn't realise that the stars had vanished and now we were both in a garden, by the edge of a fountain.

"Where are we?" I asked, looking around.

"Back at the manor. I have a very dear memory connected to this fountain."

Something on her face made my heart struggle. The sad look? The nostalgic smile? Or maybe it was the way she played with her finger in the water without even disturbing it.

"Leah?"

"Hmm?"

"What am I supposed to do? Some time ago, you said you need my help, but I don't know how."

The magic dissipated instantly. We were back amid the stars, and I was dressed in my regular clothes.

"I will need you to be there for me. More than anything else, I'll need a friend."

"But how am I supposed to do that? We are separated by about two hundred years, and it looks like I can't travel whenever I feel like it, and you can't get in touch with me when you need me. So, tell me, how am

I supposed to be there for you with such a great wall between us?" I blurted out, frustrated, in one breath.

"But you can, Scarlett," her tone was understanding. "There is only one condition you must fulfill. Keep the connection open at a minimum level, at all times."

"But how can I do that? And especially how can I do it without constantly having red hair?"

She grabbed my head between her palms and stuck her forehead to mine. Her skin felt cold and soft, and I felt as if a weight has been lifted off.

"I've learned a lot since I came here. That should help."

"What did you do?"

"A slight adjustment," she told me, smiling. "The ability you inherited has not been used for several generations, and that is why your body didn't know how to adapt. That's why you felt exhausted, and that is why you had a hard time releasing the flow at will."

"I think I understand most of what you tell me, but what about my hair?"

"Your hair will have a constant reddish glow, but nothing more as long as the energy used will be minimal. But you don't have to worry. Laura has something for you."

"Oh! You are right; Laura said she would help me."

"I just hope to hurry; she doesn't have much time on her hands."

"What is that supposed to mean?" I asked, confused.

"It is not for me to say, but you'll find out when the time comes."

Before I could say anything more, the view changed. We were in a small, dimly lit room. In one corner, behind us, was one of the maids.

"Go to her, Scarlett . . ."

I approached the young woman and noticed that it was Leah. A younger Leah, with red cheeks, who was applying a cold compress on her right forearm.

I looked confused from one to the other. The latter did not seem aware of our presence, and the other did nothing but watch as it changed its compresses, revealing briefly some long red cuts that bled here and there.

"What's the meaning of this?" I looked in horror. "What happened?"

"It's just the beginning . . ."

Closing her eyes, she became unseen, and I felt drawn into the viewer's place inside Leah.

"Scarlett, you scared me!" Leah jumped.

"Were you waiting for someone else?" I tried to joke, though I'm not sure how convincing I was.

"No, not at all." She laughed.

"Leah, what are those marks on your arm?"

"I broke something, so I had to be punished," she said dismissively.

I bit my tongue to say nothing while she spread some kind of ointment over the wounds, and wrapping them in a bandage, she let her sleeve down.

"Why are you angry?" she asked as she walked out of the small room, and down the corridor.

"How often does this happen?"

"Not too often," she tried to avoid the answer.

"How. Often? And don't try to lie to me because I can feel when you do it," I warned her.

"Once, maybe twice a week, but that's only my fault since I'm so clumsy."

"Oh, Leah . . . why did you want to come back to this place? Now you could've been somewhere far away, safe."

"I'm happy here."

I felt that she wasn't lying, and that is precisely why I couldn't understand. How could she be happy in a place where she was physically punished even for the littlest mistake?

For one thing, I was sure; Leah was strong.

We stopped in front of a pair of black doors.

"That's not . . ."

"It is. These were Lady Jubilee's rooms," she said hesitantly. *"The Earl ordered the doors to be painted black and that no one is allowed to enter. Nobody but me, who has to clean them."*

Before we entered, I heard a male voice shouting at Leah, and from behind a corner, no one other than Chance appeared.

"Leah, can you give me control for a little?"

"Sure, but what do you want to do?"

"You will see, only for a few minutes, please."

I didn't even finish the sentence when I felt the door handle in the palm of my hand, and the marks on my arm, burning and pulsing. I looked at Chance once, then entered the room, leaving the door open for him to follow me. I could say he fell straight into a trap.

He came into the room, closing the door behind him, but he didn't get to turn before I gripped the collar of his coat, and pushed him as hard as I could, slamming him against the door. I heard Leah screaming somewhere at the back of my mind, but I was too angry to care. With his big eyes and opened mouth, I could read the surprise on his face, but I couldn't care less. He'd made a promise and broke it.

"Scarlett! Just as delightful and violent. What's the reason for this lovely meeting?"

"You are a liar," I said between gritted teeth, squeezing the fabric in my clenched fists while pushing him harder against the closed door. "I can't believe I trusted you." My blood was boiling, and my hand was throbbing even harder because of the effort.

"Scarlett!"

"Stay out of this, Leah! Please, stay out of this!"

His tone changed from surprised and playful to serious, grimacing.

"Scarlett, what is going on? You don't make any sense."

"Of course, I don't . . . You promised! You promised you would take care of Leah! You broke your word!"

He grabbed my hands to stop me from pushing, but when he touched my hurt arm, I felt like a thousand needles pierced through my skin at the same time, making me scream in pain. With teary eyes, I pulled back, putting some distance between us.

"Scarlett, what's wrong?" he asked, worried.

"Just stay away, don't come near me!" I shouted.

Ignoring my words, he came by my side, holding my face between his hands, so he could look in my eyes.

"Tell me what happened." Despite his pleading voice, this wasn't a request.

His hands smelled pleasant, like paper and ink, but this wasn't the time to be distracted. Aggressively, I pulled up the sleeve and undid the bandage, revealing the wounds on my forearm.

"You promised . . . you promised you won't let anything bad happen to her."

Sadness and guilt brushed his face, disarming me of all my anger, leaving behind only the disappointment of a broken promise.

"Chance, what is happening in this house?"

He didn't have an answer to give me, but he pulled me to his chest, hugging me and stroking my hair. I could hear his heart beating strongly, and I could feel mine beating in the same rhythm. We stayed like that for minutes, but in the end, he had to leave.

"Until next time, my sweet Lady."

With a small bow, he vanished behind the black doors. It felt weird when he was doing that, is not like I was some sort of big shot.

Leah started giggling, reminding me of her presence. Now that I thought about it, it was kind of awkward that the whole scene happened the way it did, but it was too late to change anything. I retreated, giving Leah back the control over her body; I'd made enough stupid things, for now.

"You like him . . .," she said friskily.

"Don't be silly . . ."

"Then, you hate him? But I don't think you hug someone you hate the way you did."

"I don't hate him." I rolled my eyes

Hearing my answer, she started chuckling again, while wiping the dust.

I didn't hate him, and most certainly, I didn't like him; at least not in the way Leah implied. It would have been stupid to let myself be captivated by someone who lived in a different century. Who cared about his diamond-shaped face and the firm, sculpted jawline; his copper-brown eyes and the short hair of the same colour; his broad chest; or his strong arms wrapped around my shoulders . . . or his warm smile . . .?

Stop it, Scarlett! These kinds of thoughts aren't helpful.

"Scarlett . . ."

"I don't like him!" I snapped unintentionally, but luckily, Leah behaved like she didn't mind me.

"Can you hear it?"

"Hear what? I can't hear anything."

"A ticking. A clock? But there isn't one in this room."

"What are you talking about?"

She walked to the farthest corner of the room and glued her ear to the cold wall.

"It's coming from here."

"Leah, I can't hear anything. Leah?"

Without answering me, she began to feel the wall. Gently moving her fingers on its surface, she noticed that the wallpaper was cut with a very thin blade, making it almost invisible. She tried to push it, and to my surprise, a piece moved, leaving a mouldy smell entering the room.

"I don't think that's a good idea."

Leah grabbed a candle and stepped into the dark tunnel.

"Leah, we shouldn't be here." I raised my voice.

As if she couldn't even hear me, she continued to advance as if hypnotised toward an unknown destination.

As it deepened, the tunnel split a few times, forming a maze that may be stretched for miles, but nonetheless, Leah continued her journey without any hesitation, as if led by an invisible force.

The whole place was giving me the creeps. The stone walls seemed ancient, but even so, there wasn't any sign of any living creature through the cold and damp tunnel; no sound of rodents, no spider canvas, and especially not even a trace as if someone had passed through there for tens or maybe hundreds of years.

A bad feeling lingered at the back of my head.

The steps led us to a room made entirely of white marble. Columns, like those of Greek temples, and later taken over by the Romans, supported the high ceiling, from where, carved in ronde-bosse[1], Zeus looked down. The walls were adorned with similar sculptures, which viewed in the right order, told a long-lost story. But this was not the time to let myself be distracted by the place's architecture, as Leah moved with small steps towards the centre of the room.

On a pedestal, in a glass box, sat a small pocket watch, which seemed to throb, resonating at every step Leah made toward it.

"Leah, you'd better stop now."

I could feel her heart beating, and her breathing became heavy.

"Leah!"

She reached for the small object, and when her fingertips touched the cold material . . .

"LEAH!"

. . . an overwhelming pressure was released suddenly, throwing us all the way to the columns which began to vibrate.

"We need to go back. Now!" I yell at her, frightened.

She got up from the ground, but instead of taking it toward the tunnel, she approached the box again, which now had a small crack.

"Leah! Stop it!" I kept shouting.

She stopped in place for a few seconds, struggling within whether or not to touch the box again, but before she could make a decision, thin threads of electricity began to quickly cross the transparent material of the box, bursting into a lightning storm that hit the walls and ceiling.

Suddenly, I woke up in control, and without thinking, I turned on my heels and fled to the tunnel, trying to ignore the sound similar to the chirping of a thousand singing birds made by the force with which the lightning struck the air.

I didn't stop running until I got back to the room where we were safe.

When the thin soles of the shoes touched the room's carpet, my knees gave way, and I rolled to the floor, fighting to regain my breath.

Sudden pain in the back of my head made me lose consciousness, but before that, I saw clearly in front of me a pair of shoes and some black trousers . . .

. . . and a cold, gruff voice said . . .

"I found you . . ."

Chapter 13

I looked confused at the little twine hanging between my fingers. I didn't know what to expect, but it certainly wasn't a friendship bracelet. I glanced at Laura, who was sitting in front of me, avoiding my eyes, squeezing her right arm absent-mindedly.

"I know it doesn't look like much, but it should do the trick, at least for a while."

"For a while?" I tilted my head, puzzled.

"Sorry, sweets, but my powers are limited."

Trying to ignore her continuous disconcertedness, I asked.

"So, how does it work? I tie it on my wrist, and that's it?"

"Well, more or less. You need to fix it in your hair."

"That's it?" I raised my eyebrows.

"That's it."

The thin twine, made out of silk, had the same colour as my hair, so it shouldn't stand out. I tied it on a hair strand at the back, making sure it wasn't visible. Checking myself in the mirror, my hair looked completely black, without the reddish glow caused by the constant energy flow. I arranged a few more rebel hairs and turned to Laura, who had a pale smile. I had no idea what the conditions were for a successful spell, but looking at Laura's dark circles, I realised it was probably a pretty consistent effort, and she made that effort for me.

"I don't know how long the effect will last, but during this time, I hope you'll find it useful," she added.

"Thank you, Laura!" I hugged her. "You have no idea how much this means to me, and how relieved I feel knowing I have you by my side."

"You're welcome, sweets. I'll help you as long as I can." She patted my back.

Something in her voice was bothering me. She seemed; distracted?

"Are you alright?" I gathered the courage and asked.

"Yeah, just a bit tired."

I was one hundred per cent convinced that it was something more than fatigue, but if she didn't want to tell me, I couldn't get my nose in it, and besides, I had no other way to find out.

"Laura!" I called her before she managed to get out the door.

Still facing the other way, she didn't answer, but I knew she listened.

"Maybe you should go home today. You look like you're about to fall off your feet. I'll talk with the Director if you want me to, after all, you did the same thing for me not too long ago."

"I'll be fine. You don't need to worry about me."

Maybe she said that, but I couldn't help but get the

impression that if I let her go now, I would never see her again. She would disappear among the shadows as if she had never existed.

Stop it, Scarlett! Laura is just tired. She will not transform into smoke and disappear into the wind.

A week off, filled with fantasy books, hadn't helped my mind stay connected to the real world.

"Scarlett?"

Laura's tired voice took me by surprise. I didn't even realise that she was still standing by the door.

"Do you like cats?"

"Cats? Yeah, I mean not in a special way, but I don't have anything against them." I scratched my head at the random question.

"I see . . . do you mind if I come over later this evening?"

"Not at all," I jumped, excited. "I could use a bit of company."

"Thank you."

She left the workshop without adding another word.

She acted oddly, and it wasn't just my imagination. I couldn't deny that she was indeed tired, the unhealthy colour of her skin and the shadows under her eyes confirmed it, but there was something else. It felt as if something was pressing her, and if she wanted to come over, maybe she needed to talk somewhere privately, but perhaps I read too much in her behaviour. She was tired and possibly lonely. I don't think I'd ever heard her speak about her family, except for the day when I discovered her powers, yet the only thing she said then was that they were inherited through the bloodline. But if so; then why did she say she went through the period of discovery and development of powers alone? That she didn't have anyone around her? Could she really be alone?

The phone began to buzz on the desk, resonating on the hardwood like an inexperienced drummer. An email from Matteo. I think it was the first one I'd ever received from him, and I saw him so rarely that I almost forgot about his existence.

To the Department of Restoration and Classification,

Seriously?

By this email, I inform you that the date for the quarterly meeting regarding the analysis and comparison of the results of the last six months was decided for Wednesday, May 24th at 8:00 am.

But that is only three days away!

The presence of all employees of the museum is mandatory. Please confirm by replying to this email.

Respectfully,
The Secretary

I understood that it was essential to have a professional appearance, but this was way too much. Damn it; I was the only member of the 'Restoration and Classification Department', he could've used my name, mainly since he chose to use my personal email address, and not the work one. Oh please, not that it mattered anymore; I had work to do.

When I finally got home, I collapsed on the couch. It was too hot for public transportation; not to mention, the air conditioning didn't work, either. I got up with some effort and opened all the windows, letting the cold air of the evening flood the small flat.

I ran my fingers through my hair, letting the fresh

air currents caress it. I completely forgot about Laura's twine, and without wanting to, I pulled it together with a few strands of hair. Silly me, but that would've probably happened anyway when I combed my hair. Fortunately, it did not seem to be broken. Maybe than tying it would have been better to attach it with a hairpin; just in case I forget again about it.

I pulled out the phone to call Laura. She said she wanted to come over later in the evening but didn't say when. When I left work, she was already gone. We could have come together. What was the point of having to go home and then come all the way to my place? Well, apparently, Laura didn't see things the same way.

I didn't even get to dial the number before I heard a knock on the door. When I opened it, I couldn't see anyone. A prank? Busy looking left and right down the hall, I didn't notice the small fluffy animal that slipped through the open door and probably wouldn't have seen it, if it hadn't started rubbing itself against my ankles.

A small, black kitten, not much bigger than my palm. I picked him up and looked at his innocent little face, his round, green eyes and tiny, pink nose, and the red bow, tied around his neck made him look like a small, fluffy present. He was so sweet that I risked getting diabetes just by looking at him, but there was a problem; if I started getting attached, I had no chance to give up on him when I would've found him a proper home. Why do people always do this? They take in pets only to abandon them later; and why at my door? There were enough centres where they could leave him.

I sat on the couch, still holding the little fluffy being in my arms, which began to lick his paws. "Are you hungry, lil' guy?"

I wasn't expecting the half-asleep fluffiness to answer me, but I thought he would like some milk. I left him on the couch pillows and went to the fridge. Unsurprisingly, I'd run out of milk, and there was nothing else that could be given to such a small kitten. I think this required an exit to the store, but what if Laura arrived before I came back? I picked up the phone again to call her, but before I even got to unlock it, the screen lit up, receiving a message.

I'm sorry, sweets, but something urgent came up, and I had to leave town for a few days. Please take care of my little friend until I get back. I know it's a big favour, but I really need help, and I don't know who else I could call.

By the way, I know she looks small, but she's big enough to eat anything, so you don't have to worry about food.

Thanks, and I'm sorry, Laura.

Oh, so it's a girl! But seriously . . . you could bring her all the way to the door, but couldn't wait a few more minutes to explain your situation face to face?

But that confirmed my suspicion. Something wasn't right.

It didn't take long until a second message came in.

There would be one more thing . . . I didn't have time to do it before I left, but I need you to give her a name. You see, a cat that stays un-named for too long becomes a nest for spirits; not too nice ones if you get what I mean.

It doesn't matter how you name her, but it is VERY IMPORTANT to do it tonight.

With love, Laura.

Awesome! A possessed kitten is just the thing I need in my house, but how in the world am I supposed to name another person's pet?

For the third time in the last half hour, I tried to dial Laura's number but without success. Either she turned off her phone, or she had no signal. In any case, I had no means of contacting her.

I sat on the couch next to the kitten who was now fighting her tail. The little creature rolled on her back and with her tail between her teeth, reminded me of a sketch from an art atlas. Represented in ink, were three fox cubs. Two of them slept quietly in the background, but the third fought the same unsuccessful battle. The artist was unknown, but the sketch had been found in an abandoned temple in the south of Japan.

I found it hard to choose a name, but what if I let her choose one herself?

Moving to the kitchen table with a sheet of paper and a pen, I divided it into a few squares and wrote the first names that came to mind while looking at her. I turned each one into a ball, then returned to the playground.

"Okay, so these are the rules," I told her in a tone as serious as possible. "I'll let go of the papers, and you have to choose one. The one you choose will become your name."

I released the paper balls near the kitten who without waiting another second too long, jumped to attack. She ran from one to the other, without grabbing or touching any. After a few minutes of running between them, she picked her prey and attacked it with all her might. I managed to retrieve the paper before she could eat it, and opening it carefully, so as not to break it, I read aloud the name that was scribbled inside.

"Midnight! Your name will be Midnight," I told her, smiling.

As if assuming the name, she looked up at me briefly, only to yawn sleepily.

A problem was solved, for the moment. If Laura didn't like the name, she could always change it- probably.

Chapter 14

"Scarlett!"

The panicky voice that rang in my mind startled me. I subtly checked the twine in my hair, which was fortunately in its place, and the strand I held continuously over the shoulder, when I was in the presence of other people, showed no sign of changing. I moved my eyes through the small room with white walls, from the Director–who sat back in his office chair, looking relaxed–to Matteo, who drew with a marker two graphics on a whiteboard, to Silvia who was filing her nails, and up to the simple window, newly fitted, which gave view to a world of freedom. In fact, it was facing the tiny courtyard behind the museum. A yard full of useless scraps, but everything was better than the boredom that pressed me now.

"Scarlett, please!" Leah spoke again, this time even more anxious than before.

It made it almost impossible for me to focus on Matteo's presentation. I wasn't interested in any way in the profit registered in the last three months, and Leah's cries didn't help either.

"I need your help. Please, Scarlett!"

Good gods, what has happened so seriously?

"Is everything alright, Scarlett?" a timid voice, asked. "Is there something you don't understand?"

I raised my eyes from the papers in front of me and realised that both the Director and Matteo were looking at me.

"No, everything is alright. Why?" I answer a bit staggered.

"You kept frowning at the report, so I thought maybe there's something you don't understand."

"Ah, no, sorry. Everything is self-explanatory. I just have a slight headache."

"Well, if there is something you don't understand, don't hesitate to ask me. Now, if we compare the graphics from the last two thematic exhibits, we can notice a significant growth, comparing to . . .," he continued undisturbed, turning back to the whiteboard he drew his graphics on.

"Please, Scarlett, I'm begging you. I don't know what to do. You are the only one I can talk to right now."

"Calm down, Leah! What happened?" I finally answered, attempting to maintain a neutral expression.

"Something odd is going on," she said, trying to temper her tone, but still sounding scared.

"What do you mean, odd?"

"Do you remember finding that strange room?"

"Yes." How was I supposed to forget?

"Shortly after, Lord Conwell ordered me to be moved from the servant's chambers, in one of the guest rooms. I am not allowed to do anything anymore, and what's

more, no one is allowed to talk to me, and I don't know why," she let it out in one breath.

"What about Chance? You can't talk to him, either?"

"He's not here. He was sent to London a little while before all this happened," Leah said disappointed.

"Isn't there anyone else you could talk to?" I frowned.

"No . . .," she answered, sadly. *"No one at all. Scarlett, what will happen to me?"*

"I don't know, Leah. The only thing I can think of right now is that you should wait for Chance to return. I'm sure he'll be able to explain a thing or two."

"Maybe you're right, but I feel so lonely."

"I can try and visit you a bit later, though I can't say for sure what that means in your time."

"I'd love that." I felt a faint smile from her.

"Then it's settled. I'll do it as soon as I get home."

"Thank you."

The situation was, indeed, strange, and that wasn't all. Surely, there was much more hidden behind her words, after all, why would an Earl do something like that? Maybe I didn't know much about the aristocratic behaviour from that time, but I was sure it wasn't common to move a simple maid into one of the guest rooms, and not allow her to move a straw. But the fact that no one was allowed to talk to her, was way more concerning.

After another ten minutes, the meeting reached its conclusion, and as soon as Matteo thanked us for attending, Silvia hurtled through the door, leaving us baffled.

"Scarlett," the Director approached me as I collected my stuff. "Are you sure everything is alright?"

"Yes, I'm sure. Why do you ask?"

"Perhaps it was only my conclusion," he frowned his stuffy eyebrows, "But most of the meeting it seemed as if you were thinking at something else. Are you sure you're fine?" he repeated concerned.

"I'm sorry. I, indeed, have a minor headache, but that's about it."

"Is that so? Because from time to time, your whole expression changed. It looked like you were thinking about something rather important."

So much for my attempt to maintain a neutral expression.

"About that . . . I need to apologise. I kept thinking about Laura," I lied. "She acted very strangely the last time I saw her, and I still haven't managed to contact her. I just hope she's alright.

Although I was genuinely worried about Laura, I had to use her as an excuse in front of the Director. There was no way I could tell him I was in an important conversation inside my head, with a young woman who lived two hundred years ago.

"Is Laura someone from your family?" he asked me thoughtfully.

"No, no, no. I mean our Laura," I answered, confused, shaking my head.

"Sorry, but I'm not following you."

"Laura Morgan, the museum's guide." I grimaced. "She's worked here for over twenty years . . . black hair, black clothes, awfully white skin, optimistic, and super friendly. . .”

“I don’t have the slightest clue who you’re talking about, but with an image like that she certainly would fit in just fine.”

“But how can it be . . .?” The blood drained from my face, and my head started spinning.

“Matteo!” the Director shouted. “Did we ever have someone called Laura Morgan in our team?”

Matteo came closer while looking for something on a tablet. He quickly surveyed the results showing on the screen, but his answer made me more confused than I’ve ever been.

“There is no file under that name in my records–”

“Maybe you put it somewhere else,” I interrupted him, raising my voice accidentally.

“Impossible,” he answered calmly. “I just completed a full search of all the files, including the archived ones. No one worked within the museum under this name. Ever.”

My fictional headache became suddenly more real than I would have liked, causing me to bring my hand to my temple, and my eyes scrunched closed under the shock that threatened to split my skull in two. Leaning against the edge of the desk, my sense of balance seemed to have evaporated. I found myself supported from both sides. On one by the Director, and from the other by Matteo. Seating me carefully on the chair, they continued to look at me.

“How can it be?” I asked, holding my head between

my palms. "She worked here since she was sixteen. How can none of you remember her?"

"Scarlett, I don't know what is going on here, but I think it should be best for you to go home for the day."

The Director's tone was cold, and so was the look in his eyes. Both he and Matteo looked at me as if I were insane, and maybe I was. None of them remembered Laura, and her name was nowhere to be found in the employees' records, not to mention her phone was disconnected. Maybe, by the time I got home, even the kitten would have vanished.

I ran my hand over the ponytail, smoothing it over my shoulder. Wait a second; I had proof that Laura was not just in my imagination, although I couldn't say anything about it. The little twine I had in my hair was all the evidence I needed to know I wasn't crazy. Laura was real, and although for some unknown reason, the two men seemed to have forgotten her, I knew the truth; or at least some of it.

"That won't be necessary. As soon as my pain goes away, I will be able to go back to work. I just need a pill, and I'll be like new." I tried to smile, but because of the constant pain waves I felt, it appeared more like a leer.

The Director looked at me for a few seconds then left, followed closely by Matteo, throwing me a few more words over his shoulder.

"Do what you want."

When the clock in the great hall beat six o'clock, I put everything down from my hand and ran out the door. I got home faster than ever, and in the privacy of my own house, I could be as crazy as I wanted. As soon as I closed the door behind me, I pulled out the phone and dialled Laura's number.

It rung! After a few days, it finally rung!

Someone answered after the second ring, but on the other side of the receiver was not Laura, but the harsh voice of a man.

"What?" he yelled, almost breaking my eardrum.

"I'm sorry to bother you. I'm looking for Laura–"

"Wrong number..." and he closed.

Wrong number?

I double-checked the number before I called again, but the same voice answered me on the phone, this time somewhat quieter but equally rude.

"What?"

"I'm looking for Laura, Laura Morgan . . ."

"What? Do you not understand that you got the number wrong?" he barked.

"I don't understand because I have talked to her on this number before, and I checked several times before calling if I typed it correctly," I said in one breath, thus avoiding getting cut off again.

"Look, kid," he said with a bit more understanding. "I don't know what you're talking about, but I've had this number for years, and there is no Laura in this house. Do yourself a favour, and me, and delete this number permanently."

Once again, the man ended the call before I could add anything else. Confused, disappointed, and tired, I crouched on the couch, sulking.

"Oh, Laura, where are you?" I whispered toward the living room ceiling, closing my eyes.

"I'm here."

The unfamiliar voice I heard from nearby made my eyelids snap open. I looked around, startled, but there was no one besides Midnight and me. With my heart beating like crazy, I tried to tell myself that it was just my imagination, but the thin and childish voice was heard again, only from beside me.

"You're not going to faint, are you?"

Midnight sat next to me and gazed at me with her head slightly tilted to the left. Was I really losing my mind?

"How long are you going to stare?" she spoke again.

My eyes widened, and a burst of nervous laughter fled my lips. I automatically got up from the couch and put a little distance between the talkative and possibly possessed kitten and me. Why was this happening to me?

"Did you just roll your eyes at me?" I asked, huffing, forgetting for a moment the scare she'd caused me.

"Oh, so your voice came back," said Midnight

mocking me, with a straight face. "It might be easier than I thought."

"You talk?" I asked in a small voice, still unsure of what I saw and heard.

"Of course, I'm talking, I'm at my fifth life. There would be something wrong with me if I couldn't talk."

"Aha . . ."

"Is that all you are going to say?" she asked coldly. "And can you stop looking at me like I'm part of a freaks' show?"

"What are you?"

"A cat . . ."

"A sarcastic one it seems." I put my hands on my hips. "Tell me, do you know where Laura is?"

Midnight stretched, then turned her attention to me.

"Right in front of you."

"What the . . .?"

"Come on, Scarlett, focus!"

"Focus on what? First, I found out Laura's kitten speaks, and now, you're telling me you're Laura?" I waved my hands around me, gesticulating. "You are nothing like her. She's sweet, and kind, and helpful, while you are fluffy and full of sarcasm."

"Right . . . I'll try and make this simple for you. When I returned to my original form, as a cat, my character changed as well."

"What was wrong with the old one?" I asked almost pouting.

"It's not a choice, you know. Look, human personalities are ten times more complex than animal ones. Laura's isn't lost completely but highly diminished and probably overwhelmed by the actual form. So, basically, I am, and I'm not Laura at the same time."

"What do you mean? I asked, confused, sitting on the carpet in front of the couch and leaning on the edge of a pillow so that I could look at her closer.

"I mean, even though I have all of Laura's knowledge and memories, as well as those of all my previous lives, I am Midnight now."

She came near my face and placed a paw on my nose. It was so soft to the touch like it was made of velvet.

"Laura . . . I mean, Midnight," it will take some time until I get used to the change. "How come I am the only one who remembers you?"

"Because I chose you as my human, and you named me before fourteen past two in the morning."

"Fourteen past two? That's a weird time."

"That's the time I was born the first time, so no matter what I do, it's connected to that hour. For example, if you would've hesitated even more than you already did to name me and waited until the following day, it would've been too late. You would have completely forgotten Laura, and I would have had no choice but to behave like a normal cat until my next life." She stretched again and yawned. "I'm sick of this conversation, I'll take a nap."

"Hey, wait! I'm not done talking yet. I still have questions for you. Midnight!"

Curled up like a doughnut, with her back at me, Midnight pretended to be asleep, ignoring me.

Chapter 15

"You're an idiot, you know that?" the woman asked, lazily sipping from her wine glass. "You have the ambition and power to fulfil all your desires, and yet, you're messing around."

Clenching his fists, the Earl gritted his teeth, hearing the woman's whipping words. He knew what she said was accurate, but the way she said it was pissing him off. Never in his life, had he allowed someone to address him with such a lack of respect, even less a woman. He wanted to jump over the desk and sink his hands into her throat. He wasn't going to do her any harm, he just wanted to scare her good, but he couldn't. He needed her. No! He needed the information she owned.

"And what do you suggest I do?" the Earl asked coldly, leaning against the back of his desk chair, entwining his fingers in front of his chin.

"Are you serious when you're asking me this?" she scoffed at him.

"There's something I don't understand. What's in it for you?"

Waiting for an answer, the Earl measured her from head to toe, trying to place her somewhere on the social scale, but the woman was a walking contradiction.

After the careless position, with both her legs draped over one arm of the chair, she didn't seem to be any lady, but her mannerisms were perfect–except when they were alone. In the beginning, he thought she could be a high-class prostitute, with her deep and generous cleavage and the way she deceived so many naive lads, but at the same time, she had the pride of a duchess. Perhaps a spy, but with such a fragile constitution as hers, she wouldn't have survived even for a day among the beasts. He had no idea who she was or where she came from, but she knew things no one from outside his family should've known.

The woman stretched her arms above her head, and removing the hairpins, she released her dark and lustrous hair. In the position she was sitting, her locks almost reached the floor.

"I'm sure I already told you that when we met the first time," she sighed idly. "You have something I need."

"The Watch."

"Correct. But as you know, it can't be used by an outsider, so this is where you come in," she smiled mischievously, with one corner of her mouth. "I help you break all the seals, and in exchange, you will fulfil my wish, of course, after you have fulfilled yours."

"What wish?" the Earl asked distrustfully.

"Oh, but I can't tell you now," she giggled. "You'll just have to trust me."

"How can you ask me such a thing, when you're not willing to even reveal your real name?"

"Hmm . . .," she touched her lower lip with a finger, "you can call me Selene."

"Is that your given name?" he raised an eyebrow.

"Who knows? I have so many names, not even I know which one was the first."

With the empty glass swinging between her fingers, she turned her eyes toward the dark window, glancing nostalgically at the starry sky.

"You have the girl and you have the Watch, so what are you waiting for?" she asked, returning her attention to the Earl.

"The artefact is rejecting her," the crease between his eyebrows seemed even more profound than before, his eyes fixing the desk's surface. "If it keeps up that way, she might lose her life."

"And that surprises you?" Selene smirked sarcastically.

The Earl raised his face, baffled, just in time to see her rolling her eyes at him.

"You already have all the answers, so why can't you connect them? As I said earlier, only someone from your family can use the Watch, and that applies as well when it comes to the seals."

"Your point being?"

Selene rose from the armchair, her red skirts sweeping the floor and approaching the desk, she bent over it, near the Earl's face. Smiling coldly and with a dark glow in her different-coloured eyes, she whispered.

"You will have to marry her."

Chapter 16

The pain I felt coming from her made her unaware of my presence. The deep, half-healed burns covered her arms up the elbows, making her whimper as she applied an eggy-smelling oil over them. I looked terrified at the irritated wounds, which here and there looked infected, asking myself the same questions, again, and again.

Why?

Why did you come back?

Why do you insist on staying?

Why remain in a place which destroys you?

Why are you clinging to a memory which rips you apart?

"Scarlet?" she asked, feeling my nervousness.

Before I answered, I waited for a second, I wanted to make sure that when I opened my mouth, my voice would be calm.

"I'm here, Leah."

"It's been a while." She continued while wrapping a bandage over her arms, only then to cover them with a pair of long, white, lace gloves.

"How long has it been since you called out to me?"

"About two months."

So, indeed, I had no control over the moment in which I got here.

"I'm sorry, Leah. In my time it's been only a few hours."

"It's alright, don't worry about it."

"Leah . . . your arms . . ." I wished her to tell me without me having to mention it, but I could feel she had no intention to do it.

"It's not as bad as it looks," she tried to fake a smile.

"What happened?" I asked, trying my best not to snap at her attempt to appear unaffected.

"Do you remember that strange room?"

"Yes . . ."

"In that room, we found something . . . a pocket watch. You do realise what we stumbled upon, right? Chronos's Watch."

I was suspecting something similar, but hearing her say the words, made everything way more real.

"Leah, that doesn't explain what happened with your arms. How did they end up in such a state?"

"His Lordship moved it to a different room, inside the house–"

"What do you mean he moved it? When you tried to touch it, it threw lightning left and right," I interrupted her.

"Do you remember what Lady Jubilee said? It's her family's duty to protect and guard the Watch, so it's only natural that they could touch it without any issues, right?"

"I guess so . . .," I said, unsure.

"But something odd happened soon after that."

"Explain," I rushed her, starting to lose my patience.

"The marble room, the labyrinth, the tunnel, every-thing is gone. And what was the entrance in the tunnel, turned into the room's wall."

Odd was an understatement, but that's not what I wanted to know. I wanted to know what happened to her hands; why they were so damaged? And mainly who was to blame for that?

"Leah, your hands?"

"Be patient! I need to tell the whole story for you to understand."

"Then do it already!"

"You know, Scarlett, Patience is a virtue," she said chuckling.

"Yeah, well, I don't feel very virtuous today." I didn't even bother to hide my sarcasm, making Leah chuckle again. *"So, keep going."*

"He wants to activate the Watch."

"He can't!" I shouted.

"No, he can't. At least not by himself, and that's why he needs me."

"Did he tell you that?" I asked, finding it hard to believe. I didn't know much about him, but I doubted he was the type to give any explanations, even less to a maid.

"No, Lady Jubilee told me some time ago. Since I have the ability to control artefacts, I should also be able to undo the seals that keep it inactive."

"How?" I asked, interested.

"I didn't understand everything she told me back then, but the main idea was that the Watch will do it by itself. It will draw the required energy from me and will break them from inside out. But the Watch doesn't let me get near it, hence the wounds you saw on my arms."

"Wait a moment, I thought the Watch mustn't be activated no matter what."

"It mustn't be. Lady Jubilee warned me about that. She said that if I'll ever find myself near the Watch, to not give it the energy it needs, at least not willingly."

"Then, I suppose it's a good thing it rejects you, but if the Earl keeps pushing you, I'm afraid it might become a danger to your life."

"After today it won't matter anymore, because–"

A knock on the door interrupted her line of thoughts, and from behind the door, a woman spoke.

"My Lady?" she said softly.

My Lady?

"May I come in? It's time."

"Come on in, Emma," Leah answered out loud.

The door opened, and Emma stepped into the room, carrying a white dress.

"My Lady, it's time," she said again, once she got closer.

"I see . . ."

I observed, confused, the whole scene, and I knew for sure I was missing something. Emma was the one responsible for Leah since the day she put a foot on the domain. She was her superior but now called her 'My Lady'.

Without her, or Leah making another sound, she helped her put on the dress and fixed her hair.

"Um, Leah? Why did Emma just call you 'My Lady'?" I asked, starting to get a bad feeling.

"Because it is expected from her," she answered as Emma placed pieces of jewellery in her hair and around her neck.

"By whom?"

"Society, etiquette, everyone . . ."

"But what does that have to do with you?"

"You'll see soon enough," and a tear slipped down her cheek.

With a heavy sigh, Emma wiped it away, then resumed powdering Leah's face with rice flour.

"I told you to be careful, child," she said, worried.

"I know, but there's nothing I can do now," Leah's voice was bitter but determined.

"Someone will let you know when the time is near. Please wait here," Emma added, then she left without looking back.

Leah stood up from the chair, where Emma had fixed her hair and make-up and walked up to a big mirror. Her simple, white dress was a perfect fit, with short sleeves and lace gloves that hid the bandages on her hands, her hair raised in an elegant cocoon and her powdered face, made her look like a porcelain doll. She was gorgeous, but miserable, with her eyes void of any light and the corners of her mouth dropped toward the ground.

With an effort of will, she displayed a pale smile, and with a broken voice, she said out loud.

"Scarlett, I'm getting married!"

No, nope, this couldn't be happening. Leah was getting married, and with no one else but Lord Conwell.

As we walked down the empty corridor, with the veil pulled over her face, Leah was so disconnected from reality that I could hardly see or hear what was going on around. I felt like I'd gotten stuck in a sea of haze. A cold, sticky fog that reached to my bones, turning them to glass. The glimpse of the corridor, I managed to catch, seemed familiar, but that was probably because Leah had spent so many years there.

Stopping in front of a door, which today seemed more prominent than usual, we stayed there for a while, Leah being unable to turn the doorknob.

"Leah, I'm here for you." What else could I say? More than anything else, she needed support.

Her hands trembled as she clutched the little bouquet Emma had prepared and tears gathered in the corner of her eyes.

"I know," she answered, taking a big breath. Pushing

back her tears and straightening her back, she walked into the room, where her future husband was waiting. *"Thank you."*

The ceremony took place in the parlour. The poorly decorated room was clear evidence of the importance given to the event. In one corner of the room stood Chance, who was barely able to mask the grim expression on his face, and in the other corner was Emma, who had hitherto worn an impeccable mask. I realised they were holding the place of witnesses as in the room, there was no one but them and the cleric.

The cleric began the unifying ceremony of the two, but every time he spoke Leah's name, he avoided looking at her, and the vows were non-existent.

The time came to exchange the wedding rings. The Earl grabbed her wrist tightly, causing her to bite her lip to distract herself from the pain he caused her, and without bothering to remove her glove, he pushed the plain gold band forcefully on her finger.

Leah took her wedding ring as well, but before she managed to put it on the Earl's finger, she dropped it. The ring rolled all the way to the door, under her frozen eyes, settling with a metallic cling that echoed through the room. Chance picked it up and walking up to Leah, he placed it in her hand. Once the ring exchange was complete and the registry signed, the Earl stormed out of the room, followed by Emma shortly.

In all this time, Leah's eyes were stuck on the floor, not even one look at the man who was now her husband or anyone else in the room.

"It's something wrong?" I asked, feeling the fright in her soul.

"I dropped the ring," she told me terrified.

"But Chance returned it, so everything is fine now, right?"

"No. The one who drops the ring during the marriage ceremony is doomed to die long before his spouse."

"It's just superstition, Leah. You don't need to worry about this stuff. In my time, if the ring is dropped, it is said that the couple will have a happy and adventurous life, so you can't really trust these things."

"You may be right," she answered, but I could feel that my words did not manage to calm her down, not even a bit.

Chance who stayed behind to pay the cleric approached us.

"Leah, are you alright?" he asked, concerned.

"Yes," she forced a smile, looking at the floor. "Everything will be fine."

The last few words seemed more like an encouragement to herself than an answer to Chance's simple question.

"Leah, can I talk to him a bit? You could rest."

"Sure." The transition was fast, Leah hiding in the shadows of her soul.

The wounds on my arms made me feel uncomfortable, sending me waves of pain every time I moved them, but it was bearable. The golden band on my finger seemed heavier than it should have been; those were the feelings Leah left behind, however, there was something else. From the spectator's position I had been in until a few seconds ago, I couldn't realise, but something felt wrong with her body. I couldn't figure out what it was, but I had the impression there was something more than what she'd told me.

"Missed me?" I asked with a playful smile, looking up to him.

"I'd be lying if I'd say no," Chance told me honestly.

Chapter 17

"Forgive me, Julia! Forgive me, my love!" whispered the Earl, falling to his knees in front of the portrait of his late wife. "Forgive me!"

Pulling his hair and with his forehead on the cold floor, he howled like a lunatic. Taking a deep breath, he got up and, with the steps drowsed by the several glasses of brandy he had thrown down his throat breathlessly, he neared Julia's portrait.

"Soon, my love, soon," he pressed his lips to the painted canvas. "Wait for me."

He stepped out of the narrow space where he had hidden his most precious treasure and collapsing in the large chair, poured another glass. Before he drank, he looked once again at the subtle glow the wedding ring had.

As he entered the study, he jerked the wedding ring off of his finger and threw it into the fire in the fireplace, replacing it with the old, silver one from Julia.

"Soon," said he, beginning to laugh. "Soon," and emptied the glass with a single gulp.

Chapter 18

He missed me? I said it as a joke, but he answered with such a genuine look on his face. Nah, he must be just messing with me.

"*I don't think he's joking; you know,*" I heard Leah's sleepy voice.

"*What do you mean? There is no way he can be serious. We barely met twice, or maybe three times . . .*"

"*True, yet he always asks me of you.*"

Always?

"You look very cute dressed as a bride," Chance said, slowly tilting his head to one side, and smiling.

Being focused on what Leah was telling me, his voice took me by surprise. I looked at him with big eyes, aware of the blood that flooded my cheeks, but then I remembered. I was inside Leah, so she was the cute one, not me. No one could see me.

I don't know what kind of expression I showed, but Chance came even closer, and with his hand, he lifted my chin enough to look me deep in the eyes.

"What's wrong?" his voice, warm and low.

"You mean Leah is the cute one dressed as a bride," slipped my tongue.

Surprised, he stepped back a bit, pulling his hand away, the memory of his touch persisting on my skin.

"Why would you say that?" he frowned.

"This is Leah's body," I said gazing at my hands. "No matter who looks will see Leah, not me."

"But I see you."

"Liar," my bitter-sweet laughter echoed in the room, unable to understand why it bothered me so much.

"I'm not lying," he said, seaming a bit hurt. "Whenever you take over, it's you I see, not Leah.

Gods, how much I hoped it would be true, but I found it so hard to believe.

"Then tell me; what's the colour of my hair?" I asked him, well aware of the apparent differences between Leah and me."

"Dark, like the night we first met," he answered without any hesitation.

"Then, what about my eyes?" It was me who got closer to him this time.

"Brown, just like cinnamon," he smiled.

"Did Leah tell you?" I asked, frowning, still untrusting, but I wondered; did Leah actually knew?

"What do you want me to say for you to believe me?" he sighed deeply.

"I don't know. An explanation, maybe?" I shrugged my shoulders.

"Fine, but not here," his voice turned into a whisper. "Meet me in the library in half an hour. Perhaps you'll want to change into something more comfortable in the meantime."

I nodded, but curiosity had already gotten the best of me. Could he indeed see *me*?

Getting out of the wedding dress turned out to be a more significant challenge than I first expected. There were so many things to undo: buttons, ribbons, layers which had to be removed in a specific order. I began to question my ability to get redressed. I didn't want to ask for Leah's help, who looked like she'd fallen asleep.

The earlier discomfort returned in full strength, but it didn't come from the wounds on my arms, but from the back. Dumping the thin, white layer left covering me, I walked in front of the mirror.

Oh, my dear gods!

Dozens of purplish, striped marks, covered her back, darkening her white skin. I could hardly hold myself back from waking Leah up and questioning her, but there were two problems. One, if Leah would've wanted to tell me about this, she would've done it earlier, and two, even if I learned about it, there was nothing I could do, since this was not my world.

I looked for a dress which looked easy to put on and dragging back over my head the white, muslin shirt, I put a blue dress on, skipping the corset. There was no way I could figure that thing out; not without help.

Stepping out of the room, I headed straight to the library. It wasn't hard to find, but I didn't expect something so vast. The shelves fixed on all the walls, and some even arranged in the middle of the room, kept thousands of books. Somehow it reminded me of the museum's library, the difference was that this one was much more organised. I got closer to a shelf that looked ridiculously familiar. Decorated with leaves and flower carvings, it was different from the rest on the furniture in that room. I reached my hand to touch one of the leaves, but when the door opened, I pulled it back quickly.

Chance entered the room with a shadow of worry on his face, a shadow that evaporated when our eyes met.

"For a second I thought you would disappear again," he said.

"You don't get away so easily from me," I replied, smiling. "Especially when you promised me an explanation."

"Yes, about that . . ."

He couldn't finish what he had to say. Suddenly, grabbing my arm, Chance dragged me behind him. Pulling a shelf near the fireplace, it moved away from the wall. He drove me into the narrow space by sticking me with my back against the cold stone wall, and after he entered, he pulled the shelf back to its original position. The place became so small that we had no choice but to press our bodies against each other.

"What do you think you're doing?" I raised my

voice protesting, trying to push him away, but just like on the night when we met, he was unyielding.

"Shh . . . listen," he whispered in my ear, sending shivers through my body.

Just then, the library door slammed, making me jump, and Chance, tense.

From the other side of the shelf, from inside the room, two unfamiliar voices were heard; a man and a woman. The discussion seamed slightly tensed, but they didn't talk loudly enough for me to understand them. The muffled voices came closer to the shelf behind which we hid. I covered my mouth with both of my hands and felt afraid even to breathe, so we wouldn't get caught. Something was removed from the shelf; then a few seconds later, the door slammed again. Did they leave? Or did someone else come in? But on the other side was quiet. There wasn't another sound to be heard, apart from my own heartbeat.

Surrounded by darkness, I could feel his arms resting against the wall, on both sides of my head. I raised my eyes to him, though I couldn't see him when I did so, the tip of my nose and my lower lip brushed the thin skin of his neck.

The chilly, damp air made me wrap my arms around my body, desperately trying to protect myself against the cold which crept under my skin. A small movement, but Chance noticed it.

"I'm sorry," he whispered, "but I think we might need to stay here for a little while longer. I don't want to risk being caught."

He pulled me in his arms, rubbing my back to warm me up when suddenly his hand stopped on the small of my back.

"You're not wearing a corset?" he asked, surprised, his body tensing even more.

"No," I answered a bit embarrassed, whispering. "I couldn't figure it out how to put it on."

"Why you have to be so . . ." his words got lost in nothingness.

Pulling me against him even harder, his mouth took over mine. His smell, his taste, made me drunk, drawing me in even more. I could've stepped back, I should've stepped back, but it felt impossible. I wanted more. I wanted *him*. I lifted my hands around his neck, pushing my chest against his. The growl that escaped his throat lit a spark inside me, a spark that soon became a flame. He moved a hand from my back, leaving a blazing trail behind, and putting it in my hair, pulled my head aside. He broke the kiss for a while, only to move his lips from mine to the side of my neck, making my knees go soft.

Never in my life, had a simple kiss made me feel so high.

"Chance . . ."

Hearing his whispered name, he froze, and releasing me suddenly, he turned and pushed the shelf, stepping back into the library.

Looking at his broad back, getting further away in the room, I felt lonely, rejected and mostly guilty.

Just what am I doing? Do I really have to keep

reminding myself that this is not my world? That this is not my body? Or that the man in front of me will never be truly mine?

The last thought came as a surprise. I was, indeed, attracted to him, there was no doubt there, but that's where it ended. A temporary attraction, without a future.

"Scarlett!" his sudden approach made me jump. I didn't even notice when he stopped in front of me. "I am very sorry. Could you forgive me? I don't know what came over me," he continued apologetically.

"What are you talking about? It's not a big deal. You don't need to worry about it."

"Well, it doesn't look like *no big deal* to me."

When I looked at him confused, he took my hand, and with the tips of my finger touched the wet trail on my left cheek.

"It's from the light," I lied, though I wasn't sure, either, what was the real reason. "Never mind that. I think you have something more important to tell me."

"Right, I promised an explanation," Chance scratched his head. "Leah?"

"I don't really feel her, so there is a good chance that she's asleep. Is this something she's not supposed to hear?"

"Something like that. It's not that I don't trust her, it's just better, and safer for her not to know."

"Know what?" I asked puzzled.

"That I'm one of you. She has a hunch, but she has

no confirmation possibility since my talent doesn't stand-up in any way.

"And what would be your talent, more precisely?"

"I see things normal people miss."

"Such as . . .?"

"Such as, if certain individuals have any sort of power, or if they pretend to be someone else. There are people who can make you see things that aren't there or people who can make you blind to things right in front of you."

"Hypnosis? Illusions?"

"You could say that, but you see, none of this affects me. And what's even more, I can easily read a person's power level."

"So, it is true. You can really see *me*." I answered quickly, showing a wide, eager smile.

"You still doubted after how I described you not too long ago?" he asked, laughing.

"It's not like that," I turned a bit red. "It was just that I couldn't understand how you were the only person in the house who could tell the difference."

"It certainly would've been interesting to see what would have happened if an unknown young woman suddenly appeared in Leah's place, and started roaming around the house."

He laughed, pushing a strand of hair behind my ear.

"Nothing good," I said quickly, shaking my head. *Especially for Leah.*

"I don't think it's wise to linger around here any

longer," he said, looking towards the door. "After all, Leah is still not allowed to leave her chambers, and no one in the house is allowed to talk to her."

"Why?" I raised my voice, frowning.

"Most likely because of the Watch."

"You know about the Watch?" I involuntarily stepped back, my eyes widening.

"Yes, unfortunately, I know. That blasted Watch is the reason why I'm here."

"I don't get it. What do you mean because of the Watch? Aren't you supposed to be the Earl's secretary?"

"That's just a cover-up." he wrinkled his nose. "I was sent here by the Crown to keep Conwell under observation.

"Hey! Do you think it's safe to say this kind of stuff out loud?" I jumped, still trying to wrap my head around what I'd just heard.

"This house is old, and has a lot of secrets," he continued, ignoring my little protest. "You can't see them, but I can. Rows and rows of runes which spread from one corner of the room to another. They are still glowing, meaning the enchantment is still active

"Enchantment?"

"No one from outside this room can hear what happens in here. Try to imagine twenty children with trumpets and violins, and although not one of them can play, they are all playing with them, yet no one in the house can hear a sound."

"Right, but why do you need to keep the Earl under surveillance?"

"As I said, because of the Watch. Her Majesty is worried about what might happen if the artefact is re-activated, yet she refuses to give me the liberty I need to prevent a possible misfortune."

"Maybe she's unaware of his intentions?"

"She knows. I travel periodically to London with various jobs for the Earl, and at the same time, I report the situation at the manor, but the orders were clear: observe and report. Nothing more, nothing less."

"Then, why?"

"I'll tell you on the way to Leah's room. If someone notices she's not there, I don't even want to think of the consequences she will have to endure."

"But what if we meet someone on the way?" I asked a bit agitated.

"Don't worry. I told you; this house has a lot of secrets, some known only by me." He smiled mischie-vously.

He left the place where he was standing and sank further into the library, with me no more than two steps behind him.

Maybe if he hadn't shown me, I wouldn't have seen it. A narrow door, the same colour as the walls, was lost within the decor. He opened it quickly, revealing an old, dusty staircase. The light was just the one that came in from the room I was in, and it wasn't too much; the darkness seemed to absorb it.

Chance reached out under the stairway and took out a half-burned candle that he lit without a second thought.

"Come," he said, with one leg on the step, offering me his hand.

Guided by the light of the candle flickering in the beat of the low air currents, we walked through the narrow passageway leading to the upper levels of the house.

The steps were subtly rattling beneath our feet as we went on. With one hand in his and the other holding the skirt of my dress, I looked around, but there was nothing to see, only wood and stone.

"What is this place?" I asked Chance, whispering.

"This is one of the old servants' passages," he replied.

"Meaning?"

"Until recently, only high-rank servants were allowed to walk through the manor's corridors. The rest had to walk through these narrow passages. It was considered disrespectful to show themselves in front of their masters, or their guests.

"You mean they had to go through here, no matter where they had to go? No matter what they were doing?"

"Exactly," he led me around a corner.

At very least unpleasant, I thought.

"So? Why are you not allowed to take action?"

"I don't know," Chance replied, frustrated. "All I have is a simple guess."

"Such as?"

"Some time ago, during the first report, I did the stupid thing and said that the Earl has no talent. Not even a tiny trace."

"You mentioned earlier that you can see if someone has talents or not. How's that working?"

"How should I explain . . .? Have you ever heard of auras?"

"Yes. Sure, I've heard, but I thought the auras were more about emotions and things like that," I said, shrugging my shoulders.

"Yeah, but I can't see that. I don't see the normalcy in people. For example, your aura is a bright red, meaning that your talent is completely awake, while Leah's is a light blue."

"And what does that mean?" I asked curiously.

"That she has a lot of growth potential, a latent talent. We have arrived."

He said we'd arrived, but where? Around us were only the same wooden beams, paring walls, dust, and cobwebs. There was nothing to betray the existence of any entrance.

"We've arrived . . . where?" I looked at him, raising an eyebrow.

"In Leah's room." He blew out the candle flame, leaving us once again surrounded by darkness.

With a clink, Chance opened . . . a door? A panel? I didn't even know what to call it, but it didn't matter. We were where we needed to be.

I walked into the room, but Chance didn't follow me. I turned my gaze to him.

"Do you really think it's a good idea to risk being seen by someone as I leave Leah's bedrooms?" he answered my unasked question.

Sure, he was right, but I wasn't ready to say goodbye, not yet.

Probably something on my face gave me away, because Chance took a step in the room, took my hand in his, and pressed his lips on the inside of my wrist, holding my gaze, reminding me of the brief moment of intimacy we'd shared earlier.

"Till next time, My Lady."

Chapter 19

"Is there any particular reason why you look so pathetic on your wedding day?"

The Lord raised his face, looking at the woman standing across his desk. The only source of light in the room was the fire in the fireplace, every flame playing with contours and shadows of the room.

"How did you get in here?" he asked after a while, without putting down his glass.

"Are we seriously going to have this conversation every time I come here?" She smiled mischievously. "So, how is your new little wife?"

Sunk in his chair and playing with whatever was left of the cognac he had in his glass, he didn't move his eyes away from Selene, not even for a bit.

She walked around and sat on top of the desk, by the Lord's side, who finished his drink and poured another.

"Stop throwing daggers at me and listen," she commanded. "The essential condition is fulfilled, now you know what you must do."

"And what if she refuses?" he asked, shifting his attention to his drink.

"Then you will have to break her spirit." A cold smile spread across her lips.

"And how do I do that?" He stared in her different-coloured eyes.

"You're on the right path, don't worry, but you need to be a bit more aggressive."

Seeing the Earl's confused expression, Selene licked her lips, adding, "By starting with her body, of course."

Chapter 20

The slammed door of my workshop, and the quick steps that entered the room almost made me drop the clay doll I was working on. Looking up, over my protective glasses, I saw no one but the Director. With a bleak look on his face, he put both of his palms on my desk and said:

"Scarlett, I need a big favour from you."

"Sorry?" I reacted, puzzled.

"I need you to do something. Matteo is sick, and I have to leave urgently. You're the only one I can trust with this."

"Sure," I said, still confused, "what do you need me to do?"

"I want you to hold an interview."

"An interview? But I've never done anything like that before . . ."

"It's not difficult, I just want you to take a good look at the candidate and tell me if she seems to be an earnest person. I would not want to repeat the story with Silvia."

This would certainly not be very pleasant. I already knew she had no interest in this place, but such a reaction. And for what? Because a child dropped his ice cream in front of the gift shop, and she had to clean it.

"All right, I'll try. When is the interview?"

"Now."

"Now?"

"The candidate is waiting for you in the main hall." He handed me her CV and went out the door, leaving it open behind him.

I started to panic.

All right, Scarlett, you can do it. You've been to interviews before, you know how it goes; only now, you have to put yourself on the other side of the desk.

Indeed, in the main hall, a young woman was waiting for me, who seemed calm at first glance, that if she didn't crack her fingers continuously.

"Hello. You must be Kisa? "

"Ah, yes. I'm Kisa Wood, it's very nice to meet you."

"Hello. My name is Scarlett Aubyn, and I will hold your interview today. Have you ever visited our museum before?"

"No, madam, I have not."

"Then how about I give you a little tour while we talk? And please, call me Scarlett."

Well, she seemed very polite and quite honest so far. Her resume said she was nineteen, but the dark circles under her eyes and the few strains of white hair, made her look much older. She appeared to be a serious-minded person, but appearances can be deceiving.

The discussion we had didn't give me the impression

that she would be lying about anything. She didn't have much work experience, but considering her age, it was more than enough. According to her, she lived only with her brother, not having any other relatives. I didn't insist on finding out more, but one thing was clear; she needed this job.

The rest of the day passed like a breeze, which matched my plans precisely. All I wanted was to get home and jump into Leah's time.

"Midnight!" I called as soon as I entered the door.

Hearing her name, the little black furball raced toward me, almost rolling over in her haste.

"Did you bring my crunchy treats?" she looked at me with her big, green eyes glowing with excitement.

"Ah," I slapped my forehead, "I completely forgot. Sorry, Midnight." I bent to pick her up.

She stopped in the middle of the way, turned around, and pointing her tail as high as she could, walked in the opposite direction, mumbling.

"Sure. No problem. Maybe next time you'll forget to feed me or change my litter."

I froze for a few seconds. It was to be expected for her to get upset, but the attitude . . . that I was still getting used to. At times, I still found it hard to believe that this palm-sized kitten with the attitude of a queen, was the same person as sweet, friendly, and always helpful Laura. But those were thoughts for another time, now I only wanted to get to the other side.

Putting my stuff away and quickly fixing something to eat, I rushed to the bedroom and jumped in bed without bothering to take a shower. I might as well take one when I came back.

I closed my eyes and opened myself entirely to the energy flow. I could feel it surging in every corner of my body, throwing me away, back to . . . my room. Well, that's not right. Breathing in slowly, pushing away today's stress, I relaxed my body and thought of the past. The manor, the little shack in the woods, the always cheerful Leah, Chance with his dependable nature and warm smile, all these were vivid in my mind, but when I opened my eyes, I was still in the same place.

"What the hell happened?" I shouted, frustrated.

"She won't let you in," Midnight struggled to climb the bedside.

"What do you mean?" I asked frowning.

"What I mean is, Leah, as a host, has the power to let you in or not. If she doesn't want you to be there, you have no way to get in. Simple."

Midnight wasn't joking. Somehow, I could tell, but her words only made me more concerned for Leah's safety.

"This can't be good," I said more to myself. "Are you sure there isn't something I can do?" I looked Midnight straight in the eyes.

"Not that I know of. The only option you have now is to wait. I suggest in the meantime, you take a shower, you smell like something that died three days ago."

How rude . . . but she was probably right. The chemicals I worked with smelled kind of funny.

I jumped out of bed and went straight to the shower, with Leah still on my mind. And not only her, but there was also one more person I wanted to see, perhaps the one I wanted to see most.

I shook my head, dismissing the troubling thought, but it was a truth I couldn't ignore for much longer. I was attracted to him. No, I was falling for him. Despite living in different eras, despite me being a guest in someone else's body, despite that I could count on the fingers of one hand the number of times we'd met, I was falling for him, and just being next to him in Leah's body soon would not be enough for me anymore.

Leaving the hot water run, I sat in the shower, bringing my knees to my chest.

I am so pathetic, I said to myself. And a single tear slid from the corner of my eye, losing itself among the shower's steady stream.

Slightly dizzy from the heat and steam, I stepped out from the shower. Unsteady on my feet, I grabbed the sink's edge with both hands, and put my forehead against the cold, steamed, mirror. My head pulsed, my breathing became heavy, and a tension gathered at the back of my neck–getting stronger with each second, threatening to split my skull into pieces. Uselessly, I tried to regain my composure, enough to get to the bed, but when, with an effort, I straightened my back, my hair flared up, releasing all the tension in a shockwave that shattered the mirror and the shower's glass panels.

Weak in my knees and trembling, I slid to the floor, looking terrified at the shards around me.

"What have I've done?" I asked softly, my voice shaking.

"Scarlett?"

Laura? I reacted to the voice that heard from the other side of the door, feeling slightly relieved.

"Scarlett! Are you all right?"

No, that's not Laura, that's Midnight.

Without saying a thing out loud, I stretched my hand up and opened the door, letting her inside the messed-up bathroom. She looked around with big eyes, finally stopping over me, who was still seated on the floor, my naked body covered only by my, still red, locks of hair.

"Come."

That was the only thing Midnight said after seeing all this. With my body shaking, holding onto the walls, I followed her back to the bedroom.

"Get in bed."

I did as told, unable to mutter any words.

After I got under the sheets, she got on the bed and sitting on my chest, she looked at me with a stern look in her eyes.

"Close your eyes," she said a bit softer than before.

She shifted her hardly noticeable weight and pressing a paw on my forehead, she began whispering something. They were words similar to the ones Laura used on me once before, only now a warm feeling spread through my body, banishing all the fear I felt mere minutes ago.

I let myself drift away, partially ignoring Midnight's words.

"It's still too early."

Chapter 21

A soft touch on my face, a sweet kiss on my neck, and a loving whisper in my ear made me open my eyes. There was someone beside me, in my bed. Chance smiled at me and coming closer, he pressed his lips against mine. Unlike the first time when we kissed, he took his time, slowly exploring my mouth, biting my tongue and sucking on my lower lip. His hands explored my body, knowing exactly how to make me lose my mind, bringing moans and whimpers to my lips. With every touch, with every kiss, with every time he spoke my name, my body craved more; him.

With a loud noise, my bedroom door flew open, and in the darkness of my room, someone entered. Chance's warm presence disappeared from my side, as if it was never there, replaced by the cold of the night. I stayed in my bed, listening to the approaching steps, almost holding my breath.

My covers were pulled to the side and on top of me, almost squishing me under his weight, seated the nocturnal invader. The smell of alcohol was strong. Strong enough to make my stomach revolt. I tried to push him away, but when I did, a hard slap hit my face. His hand grabbed my throat, strangling me.

I grabbed his arm with both of my hands, sinking my nails into his flesh, but as I tried to fight for my life, another blow landed on my face.

"You useless wench! You dare to defy me? Your life is mine to use how I see fit!"

I recognised the Earl's voice, but to my terror, there was nothing much I could do. The lack of air was making my conscious fade away.

He removed his hand, the air invading my lungs, making me cough. Grabbing my nightgown, he ripped it, leaving me exposed. I uselessly tried to cover myself with my arms when he hit me again. Clenching a hand around one of my breasts, he pulled and twisted. I squirmed in pain.

"Scream!" He shouted, hitting me again and crushing my breast. "Scream!"

I didn't do it. Not even once. But that's when it dawned on me. These were not my reactions, but Leah's.

Getting off of me, he grabbed my legs and pulled me on the floor. I managed to get on all fours and tried to run away, but he grabbed my hands and twisted them to my back, pushing my face against the hard, cold floor. Pushing aside what was left of my nightgown, he positioned himself behind my back.

"No! Don't! Please don't!" Leah's voice was heard for the first time.

"You dare to give me orders?" He roared and. . . .

I vaulted up, screaming, in the middle of my bed, tears streaming down my face. Confused, I looked around, only to find myself in the safety of my own bedroom. Gripping the sheets in my fists and quivering hard, I couldn't shake off the atrocious scene I'd just witnessed.

"I need to go back! I need to go to Leah!" I said out loud. "But," I continued a bit disheartened, "what if I can't?"

Midnight! She did something earlier and sent me there.

"Midnight! Where are you?"

"What are you shouting for?" a grumpy voice said from next to me. "Honestly, no one can sleep in this house."

"Midnight, what you did earlier, can you do it again?"

"No, I can't."

"Why not?"

"Because I used the bit of magic I managed to gather, to pull you out of shock and fix your bathroom before you have a meltdown. Now, if you want something, do it yourself!"

She turned her back on me and went back to sleep.

She was right, again, this was something I had to do by myself. Falling back on my pillow, I closed my eyes and left myself to the mercy of the energy waves.

My body became light, attracted in the direction of the musical notes that floated in the air, growing louder. I was in someone's arms, spinning, dancing, and stumbling here and there.

"Scarlett," I heard Leah's voice.

"Leah! Are you alright?" I started.

"Take it easy, Scarlett. Yes, I'm fine. Why wouldn't I be?"

"But, the Earl. . .. He barged in your room at night, and–"

"You know, you got here just in time for dance lessons," she chirped, deflecting the subject. Once again, she refused to talk to me. But then again, what could I possibly do? The only way was to play her game if that's what made her happy.

"Dance lessons? How come?" I asked, confused.

"We are hosting a masquerade! Meaning, I will have to dance."

"Oh, wow! But why?"

"I'm not sure, but I'm tired now. How about we swap places for a little while?"

"Sure, I don't mind, but I can't really dance."

Before I could manage to finish the sentence, I was already in control of her body.

"Welcome back, My Lady."

I raised my eyes towards the familiar voice, meeting Chance's warm smile.

"Shall we continue to dance?" he asked, getting me to realise I wasn't moving.

"I can't really dance," I said a bit embarrassed.

"It's just a waltz, it's not that hard. All you must do is follow my lead. What do you say? Would you like to try?"

"Alright, but don't complain if I step on your foot. I warned him jokingly."

"I wouldn't even dream of complaining."

He put one arm around my waist and with the other, held my hand.

"Put that hand on his shoulder." Leah intervened.

I knew that; I wasn't a complete idiot, but as soon as I did it, he pulled me against his chest, holding me tight.

"Aren't we a bit close?" I asked as the blood rose up to my cheeks.

"On the contrary, I would say we are not close enough."

I looked at him with big eyes. I couldn't tell if he was joking or not, so I changed the subject.

"So, what's with this upcoming party? Something that needs to be celebrated?" I asked while Chance spun me in big circles, avoiding my clumsy steps.

"Just the usual social expectations."

"I see. In that case, shouldn't Leah be the one to exercise?"

"She did until you got here. And she's quite a fast learner if I may add."

Leah giggled, and I smiled.

"He wanted to dance with you."

"But why? It's not me who will attend the masquerade."

"Precisely. There is no guarantee you will be here then, so he wanted to take the chance whenever it showed up. That's why he volunteered to be my tutor."

"I still feel like I'm missing something."

Leah just smiled but didn't say anything else.

Our dance came to an end, and by a miracle, Chance's feet were still in one piece.

"My Lady," Chance bowed in front of me.

"Good Sir," I answered in the same way, giggling.

"Would you do me the honour to accompany me in the garden?"

"I would love too."

He offered me his arm, and, of course, I accepted it. We stepped outside in the sun, and he led the way along the unfamiliar stone paths, by the fully bloomed rose bushes.

"There is something I've meant to ask you for a while, but there were always other things going on," I said

"Well, ask me. I promise to answer as sincere as I can."

"Your name . . . I've never heard a name like yours before. Even in my time, it's not common, and I presume neither is here."

"That's an easy one. My parents tried to conceive for many years without any results. They were far past their youth when my mother found out she was pregnant with me. When I was born, and my father learnt he had a son, he said God blessed him with the chance to raise the next head of the family, and so, he named me Chance. But the real surprise came one year later when my mother got pregnant again, he snickers. No one expected for a second miracle, but it happened, and my sister was born."

"Oh, you have a sister. Where is she now?"

"She's living in France with her husband and two children."

"I see; you must miss her a lot."

"We were close, but we write to each other as often as we can, so everything is fine."

"Ask him if he has a lover," Leah said, curiously.

The idea made me a bit nervous, but I wanted to know as well.

"Do you have someone you're interested in?"

"Yes," he replied without delay.

The answer brought with itself a heavy weight on my chest, but what was I so surprised for? It was only natural for him to have someone, after all, this was his world.

"Ask him to tell you more," she pried furthermore.

I, for one, wasn't so sure if I wanted to know, but my tongue got ahead of my brain.

"Oh, is that so? Tell me about her." My voice sounded a bit cold, but he didn't seem to take notice.

We stopped by the fountain, and releasing my arm, he stepped in front of me.

"She's beautiful and feisty. She has an answer for everything. She's fun to be around, and she cares about those around her," he told me, looking at me and smiling.

It would've been better if I never heard all this because now, I knew how wrong I was. I wasn't falling for him, I already loved him.

"Sounds like quite a catch. I hope you will be happy together." I forced a smile, although unable to look him in the eyes.

He cupped my face between his hands and lifting it so our eyes can meet, he whispered.

"I'm talking about you," and he pressed his lips against mine, sealing with a kiss the words he'd just said.

Yes, it was true.

I loved those amber eyes, the short hair of the same colour, his warm smile, and the way he looked at me, but we couldn't be together. It was impossible. I was a visitor in someone else's body, and he lived dozens of years before I was even born. And yet, here we were, in the garden where anyone could see us, kissing.

"Leah, forgive me. It's your body, but I–"

"It's all right, Scarlett."

"Is it, Leah? Truly is it? And what about you? What about how you feel?"

"It's all right because I can tell how much you care for one another. We realised that these are the only moments when you can be together, even if only for a

short while, so he asked my permission to kiss you, at least once. For me it's a bit late, but I would love if you could be happy for as long as possible."

I felt heartbroken for her. Being forced into a life she never wanted; she could only witness the happiness of others. I could feel my eyes tearing up, tears of joy and sadness at the same time. When our lips finally split, I turned my back to him and lifting my skirts, I entered the fountain next to us, letting the cold water wash my hot tears. I didn't want to let him see me cry, I had my dignity.

"What do you think you're doing?" he asked, amused.

"I'm cooling off. It's scorching today," I said, but without facing him.

"And what does Leah think about you destroying her dress?"

"She's laughing out loud."

And it was true. Leah was laughing so loud I could hardly hear my thoughts. She laughed so hard, she made me laugh as well.

"Good, because I haven't seen her even smiling for quite some time. Now I suggest you get out of there before you catch a cold. I don't know how medicine is in your time, but here it leaves ugly marks."

"I would, but I can't."

Chance looked at me, confused.

"My dress is too heavy. I don't even think I can stand up."

Now it was his turn to burst into laughter, and with a big step, he entered in the fountain next to me.

"What are you doing? You'll get wet, too," I raised my voice, surprised.

"I'm saving a damsel in distress."

He pulled me out without any effort, and still holding me, we watched the water flowing from our drenched garments. Slowly, he let me back on the ground, but his arms stayed on my waist a little while longer. We started laughing, but the fun ended when a powerful, authoritative voice thundered in our direction.

"Leah!"

It only took a moment for my whole body to commence shaking, my knees weakening, and my stomach curling. I was too scared to lift my gaze from the ground, to look in the face of the one who shouted, but these were not my feelings but Leah's.

That was enough for her to push me back, where I could only be a spectator.

"What's the meaning of this?" the man spoke again, who was now standing in front of her.

With one step, Chance stood between the two and with a tone of false courtesy, intervened.

"Allow me to explain, My Lord. I needed the lady's advice in a delicate matter regarding my sister, but because of the heat, she got dizzy and fell into the fountain. As you can see, I pulled her out."

"Is that so . . .?"

Terrified, she could only nod briefly with her head, but in the moment he clasped his hand on her arm, squeezing it tightly, Leah pushed me back, with one last effort before passing out.

Chapter 22

Sleep seemed to have left me completely. Feeling restless, I got off my bed and headed to the kitchen. Opening the cupboard, I came face to face with a cruel reality–I'd forgotten to buy coffee. Without any shops open at 5 a.m., and no gas station nearby, I let out an exasperated groan.

Awesome way to start my day!

Lingering around the living room any longer was pointless with nothing for me to do so I might as well take advantage of the early hour's calmness and head to work. The tube was almost empty, a welcome change from the daily hustle.

Unlocking the museum's door, I tossed the keys in my bag and set the course towards the staff kitchenette. It didn't take long for the small room to be filled by the sublime coffee aroma. A cheap one, but it made absolutely no difference to me. I had coffee, and that was all that mattered.

On my way to my office/workshop, I didn't even bother to open the lights, satisfied with the few rays entering through the windows from the streetlights in front of the museum. I couldn't seem to figure out when I became so comfortable in this place. I could walk around with my eyes closed and still find my way without destroying anything. I wouldn't try it at home, though.

I reached my hand out to open the door but stopped midway, frowning. A strange sensation hit me, making me freeze in place for a moment. A dark, blood-like substance marked the slightly open door of my workshop, and the doorknob, still looked wet in the dim light. Taking a few steps back, I pressed a switch, turning on the lights in the corridor.

The velvety matter around the doorknob was blood, indeed, but that wasn't all. Here and there, along the same corridor I came, drips of blood stained the floor, leading inside my workshop. Juggling with my phone and coffee, I struggled to make a decision.

Call the Police? The ambulance? The Director? God-damit, there wasn't supposed to be anyone here!

A painful whimper coming from inside the room, got my attention. Placing my coffee mug on the floor, I stepped cautiously closer to the door. Pushing it softly, I expected some sort of animal to run past me at any moment, but it didn't.

Turning on the light, my heart jumped at the sight of the figure crouched in a corner, between books. With his knees gathered to his chest, hands covering his head, shaking and breathing unevenly, old man Gregor stared at me with a haunted look in his eyes. There was blood on both of his hands and on his face. I rushed to him, but as I got closer, his eyes became even larger and grabbing anything he could, he threw them at me, shouting.

"No! No! Stay away from me! You monster! Monster!"

"Gregor, it's me, Scarlett," I tried to calm him down, barely dodging a box of bloodied tissues.

"Monster! You won't get me!" He screamed like mad at the top of his lungs. "You won't get me like the others! Stay away!"

"Listen to me! There is no monster, you are safe here!" I tried to get closer, but I wasn't prepared for the challenge. Flying towards me, a massive book bounced off my forehead, jerking me back.

"Don't come near me, you human-faced devil!"

"Gregor, look at me!" I raised my voice enough to cover his. "It's Scarlett, remember? We work together. You are safe here."

As if some sort of fog lifted from his eyes, he dashed towards me and grabbing my shoulders, he whispered terrified.

"Scarlett, you need to get out of here. They are not human, none of them are."

"What are you talking about? Who are you talking about?"

"They will come for me. I set my foot in their nest. He raised his hands above his head once more, as if protecting himself from some unseen forces. They will come for both of us! They will turn us to nothing! The curse will get us!"

Crouching once again on the floor, with his hands wrapped around his knees and rocking his body back and forth, he kept mumbling and whimpering.

I stepped out from the room, leaving the door opened behind me, and while rubbing the sore spot, now swollen, where the book had hit me, I called the Emergency Services, then the Director. It was going to take a while for any of them to arrive, so the only thing I could do was keep an eye on Gregor.

To my surprise, it didn't take longer than ten minutes for everyone to arrive. The paramedics took him to the hospital as fast as they could, and the police searched the place but couldn't find any signs of intrusion.

"Scarlett, are you alright?" The Director joined me in front of the building, looking at the bloody marks on my blouse. "Why are you waiting outside?"

"Yes, I'm fine." *Psychically exhausted, but fine.* I added to myself. "I didn't want to hinder the officers, so I thought I should wait here until they finish."

"Very thoughtful of you."

"What about Gregor? Is he going to be fine?" I asked, looking at the Director's face, expecting him to share my concern.

"He is in shock, but I suppose he'll be fine." He shrugged his shoulders, relaxed, as if it didn't matter, but then, looking in the direction the ambulance left, he asked. "Did he say anything?"

"Sorry?"

"Did he said anything that didn't sound like complete madness?" he repeated, moving his eyes back on me, uselessly trying to mask the tension on his face.

"No . . . he didn't say anything. Just some non-sense."

"I see—"

"Excuse me, Miss?" A police officer approached me, interrupting whatever the Director wanted to add.

"Um, yes?" I respond, facing the young man.

"I will need a declaration from you. Can you follow me, please?"

"Yeah, no problem."

I took a few steps when the Director called my name. I looked at him, curious.

"If you remember anything, make sure you tell me."

"Sure."

There was no way I could concentrate on anything. Police were still roaming around, the Director was coming and going without saying a thing, and the dried blood stains covering my door and workplace distracted me constantly. Maybe there was a quiet place in all this madness. Picking up a few files, I made my way to the library. Taking back the old ones and getting something new to read, should be enough to take my mind off of what happened just a few hours ago.

By the looks of it, I wasn't the first one to enter that room today. Some of the shelves were moved, some boxes upside-down, files were spread everywhere on the floor, and here and there blood marks, just like along the corridor, just like in my office. Curiosity got the best of me, and following what looked like a trail, I ended up facing a wall. The little drops looked like they suddenly stopped. And so would've I, if only I hadn't heard before that behind that "wall", behind that entrance that was made to look like a wall, was supposed to be the building's electric panels. I was tempted to open that door. I felt the urge to see what made Gregor go beyond that place, and most importantly, it felt like something on the other side was calling me.

I put my hand on the hidden door, millimetres away from what looked like the painting of half a hand, made in blood. Before I could push it, Leah's voice echoed in my head–*Stop!*

I jerked back, blinking a few times.

"Leah?" I tried to call her, but there was no answer.

Softly, I rubbed my temples and tried to clear my mind. This was a stressful morning, nonetheless, so maybe I could ask the Director if I could go home and recover the lost hours on a different day.

But as I turned from the wall, like a frozen statue in the middle of the door, the Director observed me with a dark, grim expression on his face.

"You can go home now." He gritted his teeth, struggling to keep his composure.

"Sorry?" I asked, unsure of what I heard.

"We are closed for today. So, you can go home early."

I was about to ask something, but he cut me off before I could open my mouth.

"Now!" he shouted, his face turning bright red and a vein pulsing violently on his forehead, looking like it was about to pop.

Surprised and slightly frightened, I dropped the files I was still holding, and without looking back, I ran around him and out the door. Once in my office, I grabbed my bag and stuffing all my belongings in it, I left that place as fast as I could.

Chapter 23

"Why are you home so early?" Midnight came before me when I got home.

Dropping my bag on the floor and throwing myself face-down on the couch, I left out a grumble, muffled by the soft pillows.

I didn't move until Midnight's small paw touched the side of my face.

"Hey, are you alright?" she asked me a bit concerned.

I got up, sitting properly, and after a deep sigh, I told her everything that happened. About Gregor, how I found him bleeding, terrified, and on the brim of madness. About the Director, who at first looked like he didn't care, but then chased me out.

She looked at me, listening patiently to everything I had to say, then shaking her head, she spoke. "You really are a silly one, aren't you?"

"Well, sorry for being silly," I responded, unable to contain my sarcasm, "but I have limited experience with weirdness, alright? How about you enlighten me?"

"As always." She continued, unbothered by my tone, "Gregor always suspected something, but he never managed to quite put his finger on *it*. He's right.

They're not human. They may look and act like such, but–"

"Who are you talking about?" I interrupted her, confused.

"Your boss and Matteo," Midnight said with a straight face.

"Should I get someone to check up your head?" I continue, raising an eyebrow. "Okay, let's say they're not human, but then what are they?"

"That, I don't know," she said after a little break.

"Yeah, that surely clarifies a lot . . ."

"Well, excuse me, for I have failed you, My Queen," she said scornfully. "How about you keep your mouth shut for a minute and listen?"

"Sorry," I replied, taken aback by her sudden, yet not undeserved lash.

"Energetically speaking, one of them is nothing, while the other is a lot." I opened my mouth to say something, but when Midnight frowned at me, I closed it back and swallowed my words, while she kept going as if nothing happened. "What I mean is–every human has a unique energetic footprint. Matteo has none; he's blank, while the Director has a mix like he's more people in one."

"I am so confused right now." I shook my head.

"Figures." Midnight rolled her eyes.

"Okay, but aren't you guys, like part of the same, how should I call it? Community?"

"Listen, it's true that by some degree we are all involved in the mystic side of the world, but as an unwritten rule, as long as they don't disrupt my lifestyle, I have no reason to pry in their business."

"I guess that makes sense." I scratched my head. "But there is one thing that still bothers me."

"What?"

"Do you remember that fake wall in the library? You told me that's where the building's electric panels are."

"Of course, I remember. What about it?"

"Gregor said at some point that he discovered their nest, and because of that, now they will come for him . . . and me." I shrugged my shoulders. "I realise that maybe it was nothing but mad-talk, but there were a lot of bloodied marks around that entrance, so maybe, he really found something in there?"

"Impossible." Midnight stretched and yawned.

"How can you be so sure?"

"Look. I've seen that door open several times, and it's nothing in there but wires. Whatever he saw. It's most likely not there. But if you're so curious, why don't you ask him yourself?"

"Maybe it's not such a bad idea to pay him a visit. If his mind cleared, even slightly since morning, perhaps he'll be able to explain a bit better what he's seen and where."

"Right. You do that, and I'll go to sleep."

"You always sleep." I smiled.

"No! I also eat and play. I'm a growing kitten, what more do you want from me?"

"Nothing," I said, laughing.

Just then, a loud knock on the door made both of us jump.

"Are you expecting someone?" I asked Midnight jokingly, but she didn't answer. Her whole body tensed, and her ears perked up, listening for every movement on the other side of the door.

The knock was heard again, but even louder this time. I got up from the couch and headed to the door when Midnight grabbed my trousers and climbed as fast as she could on my leg.

"Ow, ow, ow! There's skin under the fabric, you know!" I looked at her reproachfully.

"Sorry," she whispered. "Just take me with you."

I held her to my chest with one hand, and with the other, I opened the door.

"Took you long enough."

I ignored his snooty comment, as I couldn't wrap my head around how, out of all people, he was at my door.

"Jared! What a surprise!"

A very unpleasant one, as a matter of fact.

"Right . . . aren't you going to let me in?" he asked, trying to push through.

"And why would I do that?" I raised an eyebrow, unimpressed by his attempt.

"If you don't want all the neighbours to hear our discussion, you'd better let me in."

"Well then, how about this. I go back inside, and you go back in whatever hole you crawled from? Yeah, that sounds much better."

"You wouldn't say that if you knew what I want to tell you," he adds confidently. "I can promise you; it will make you very happy. And I only need five minutes."

Noticing one of my neighbours poking her head from behind the door, I moved to the side and let Jared in. He was enough of a nuisance for me, there was no point to irritate the others as well.

Once inside, he went straight to the fridge and opening the door, he exclaimed, annoyed.

"Where's all my beer?"

"Down the drain. It's not like anyone in this house drinks that crap."

"Hmph, whatever." He slammed the fridge door. "I like what you've done with the place," he continued, looking around the living room.

"You mean that I cleaned it?"

"Yes. Looks like you learned a few things since I left."

"So? What is it that you want?" I asked, leaning against the entrance door, trying to suppress the anger building up inside.

"I'm moving back in."

"I'm sorry, you what?" I asked, unable to believe what I just heard.

"I'm coming back," he repeated, relaxed. "What? You thought I was going for good?"

"You left with a bag and a woman. Yeah . . . I think the message was pretty clear."

"Which reminds me," he ignored me, "you'll have to buy me my beer since you threw away the last one."

Stunned by the amount of nonsense coming out of his mouth, I didn't notice him getting closer until I heard Midnight hissing and stirring in my arms.

With an expression full of disgust, he grabbed her with two fingers by the back of her neck and raising her to his face level, he almost spit the words. "What the hell? Now you're a cat lady? This thing will have to disappear by the time I come back." And he threw her to the other side of the room.

I watched terrified as she hit the wall and fell to the ground. The seconds while she didn't move seemed like hours, but then she got on her feet, shook off her body, and ran under the couch–where she continued to hiss at Jared. Slightly relieved that Midnight seemed fine; I move my attention to Jared, who seemed disappointed by the results of his actions.

"Blasted creature!" he hissed through his teeth.

That's it! I could have strangled him there and then if that wouldn't have sent me to jail. Bashing away my murderous intent, I opened the door and grabbing Jared by the same hand he dared to hurt Midnight with, I twisted it to his back, making him scream.

"Ow! What the hell you think you're doing?"

"Visiting hours are over," I said, pushing him into the corridor and pulling at his arm once more before I let him go. "Forever."

"What the hell is wrong with you?" he shouted,

rubbing his painful wrist. "I thought you'd be happy that I came back to you."

"The only person happy to have you back would be your mother, and probably not even her, if she could see what kind of person you became." I tried to keep my tone levelled.

"Are you out of your mind? You're choosing a cat over me? Me!" he shouted at the top of his lungs.

"It's not much of a choice really." I rolled my eyes.

"This is not over!"

"Yes, Jared! It is over!" I raised my voice for the first time, and at this point, I couldn't care less that the neighbours were spying on us through their cracked doors.

"You'll be–"

"What? Sorry!" I cut him off. "Wrong. You, getting out of my life is the best thing that ever happened to me, and I intend to keep it that way. Now, how about you kindly fuck off and never come back?"

I slammed the door in his face and ran to Midnight, who was now lounged on the couch, licking her front paws.

"Are you okay?" I dropped on my knees next to her.

"Yeah. I'm fine."

"Do you want to go and see the vet? Just to make sure everything is fine?"

"No need for that. That guy throws like a baby. I've had worse than this."

"I'm sorry." I let my head fall on the pillow next to her, tears sliding from my eyes. "I'm sorry, Midnight."

"See? That's why I call you 'silly.'" She licked one of my tears. "Just make sure I don't have to see that guy ever again."

"Deal," I said sobbing.

"But somehow, it's rather funny."

"What is?" I asked, confused.

"I've never seen you that angry before, or heard you speak like that. It was rather entertaining."

"Well, I'm glad you had fun, but let's not repeat the experience."

"Agree, but he could've gotten it worse than that."

"He could have. But then I would've gone to jail, and you to an adoption centre."

"Nah. That was good enough." She changed her mind quickly.

"Thought so." I smiled and wiping my face, I asked. "Do you want to come to the hospital with me to see Gregor?"

"As far as I remember, pets are not allowed in hospitals," she said, raising an eyebrow.

"No, they are not. But you are still small enough to fit in my bag, and I thought that maybe something he would say might make more sense to you than it would make to me." I shrugged my shoulders, smiling.

"Fine. But only with one condition. Put one of those ice packs in your bag. You wouldn't believe how hot it gets in there."

Chapter 24

My patience ran low as the hospital's receptionist slowly typed all the information I was able to provide into the system.

"And what did you say is your relationship with the patient?" she asked for the millionth time.

"We work together," I said drily.

"I see, unfortunately, we can't give any details to other people unless they are family members," she continued, without raising her eyes from the computer.

"As far as I know, he doesn't have any family, and besides, I don't want information. I want to see him."

"Yes, I understand."

Are you sure about that?

"If you go through that door," she pointed to a windowless, grey double door, "you'll find the Sister in Charge. I'm sure she can help you."

"Thank you."

Finally!

I headed to the doors, and pushing hard, I entered a large room filled with beds, occupied by patients, on both sides of the area. I looked left and right, hoping to find Gregor without having to get past the Sister. I wasn't a big fan of hospitals, but one thing was clear, I wouldn't like to work in such a place.

While in some bays, patients were chatting comfortably, from others, from behind the closed curtains, I could hear groans of pain, cries, and people desperately calling for help. I wanted to get out of there as fast as possible.

From behind a curtain, a little nurse came rushing out and almost bumped into me.

"Excuse me!" we said at the same time.

"Sorry," I continued, "I'm looking for the Sister in Charge."

"The nurse's station is straight ahead and on the right. She should be there. She's the one dressed in a navy-blue uniform," she told me quickly, then ran in the opposite direction. I didn't even get to say thank you.

Indeed, I found the Sister by the station, frowning at the computer. I felt bad about bothering her, but luckily, she noticed me before I had to say something.

"Can I help you?" she asked in a worn-out voice.

"Hi. Yes, I'm looking for someone. He was brought by ambulance early this morning."

"Name please."

I gave her all the details I knew, which weren't too many to begin with as Gregor wasn't exactly the chatty type. She continued to frown at the computer's screen for another few minutes when she finally said.

"I'm afraid he's no longer in our department. He

was transferred about half an hour ago." She rubbed her tired eyes.

"Perhaps you could tell me where he was transferred to?" I asked, hopefully, but my hope was shattered by her answer.

"To the Mortuary." She looked at me for the first time.

"I'm sorry, but I don't understand." I shook my head in disbelief. "I spoke to him this morning, then he was brought to the hospital . . ."

"Where his heart failed." She motioned me to a chair next to her.

I looked her dead in the eyes, hoping to see the smallest hint of a lie. She had no reason to lie to me, yet it felt so hard to believe.

"Listen, love," she continued in a softer voice, putting a hand on my knee. "I promise you; we did everything in our strength to save him, but whatever he'd been through before he got here was simply too much for him."

"I understand." I moved my eyes to the floor. "Thank you for your time," I said automatically, and getting up from the chair, I headed to the exit.

"That was unexpected." Midnight's head popped out from my bag once we got outside. "Maybe you should sit down for a while. You look like you've seen a ghost, and I don't want you to fall over me."

Her twisted way of showing she was worried about me, put a little smile on my lips.

"I'm fine," I said softly. "I just need to process all this."

"And now what?"

"I don't know. I just want to go home and sleep."

"Sounds good to me."

Chapter 25

"How come every time I visit you; you are always in such a bad mood?"

The Earl glared at the woman for a second, then returned his attention to his documents.

"Aww, look. I even went through all the effort to come and see you, and you won't even look at me," she said in a sugary voice, mocking him. Selene waited patiently for an answer, but when she didn't get one, she became stern. "So? Any progress?"

"Two out of three seals are gone," he said without raising his eyes.

"Well, that's wonderful!" She squealed delighted. "Then, what are you waiting for? Break the third one, and you're done. After that, you can get rid of that nuisance and move on with your happy life."

"An unforeseen problem arose."

"Meaning?" the woman crossed her arms and raising her chin, she looked down to the Earl, waiting.

"It doesn't matter, it's just an insignificant delay." He rubbed the bridge of his nose, defeated.

"If it's so insignificant, then get rid of it!" Her tone was low, but it was impossible to miss the authority in it.

"I'm dealing with it!" the Earl answered, annoyed,

hitting the top of the desk with his fist. Just when did he get in the position to take orders from such a woman? "The watch is unresponsive when she's like this," he mends his tone, "but it won't be an issue for much longer."

"Good," Selene said coldly, and turning her back, she left the study like she wasn't even there.

Chapter 26

My head felt like it had a weight tied around it, making it hard to keep it straight. I was unable to focus my vision, my eyes getting foggy. A numb pain pulsed through my body, while with a bony hand, I absent-mindedly rubbed a big, round belly.

I knew too well that none of what I felt was mine, and that it was only a tiny part of how much Leah was suffering.

A gravelly voice got my attention. On one side of the room, out from my sight, I could hear two men talking.

"My lord, in all my years as a doctor, I've never seen such a grave case as Her Ladyship. I understand very well that her body rejects any type of food, but she needs to receive proper nutrition."

"I understand. I'll make sure someone will see to it," the Earl said expeditiously.

"I'm afraid that's not all." The doctor said, concerned. "The way she is now . . . I'm fearful that she won't be able to get through labour. Not to mention, there is no guarantee the child will survive until then."

No answer came after that. Nothing, but some steps and a slammed door.

"I haven't felt him move for a while," Leah said in a brittle tone.

"I . . ." was at a loss of words. Nothing I could ever say could comfort her.

"It's alright, Scarlett. It's enough for me to know I have you as a friend. But . . ." she continued, unable to keep back her tears anymore. *"I am such an idiot. I thought, even for a second that if I have my baby, I'll be able to keep going and fight against the Earl's demands. That I'll find the strength to resist the watch's energy and the physical punishments after every time I failed to break another seal."* She sobbed harder and harder, hugging her unborn child. *"I can't do it, Scarlett. I can't do this anymore!"*

"You can't give up! If you give up now, then it was all for nothing. All the hard times you've been through. For what?" But what I said were nothing but words. What did I know? I could only presume what happened to her, and there was no way to know how far or close to reality I was. She wouldn't tell me much, and I knew this was her way to keep me from worrying. After all, what could I possibly do?

She'd hit rock-bottom, that's what I could feel coming from her. Her mind and soul were in a very dark place, and the small ray of light she clung to was getting thinner by the day.

And here I was. Powerless. Unable to do a thing but stand as a witness to her nightmare.

The outside world was distorted by her anguish,

and I didn't notice the person approaching us, until, with a handkerchief, she wiped some of Leah's tears.

"It's time to eat, child," the woman said softly while patting the top of her head.

She put a small tray on her lap, but when she removed the cover, there was barely enough food for a small child, much less for a pregnant woman.

"Thank you, Emma." Leah smiled faintly, looking at the woman's pained expression. "Thank you."

"Don't thank me yet." She pulled an apple from her apron and some bread, and cutting them in small pieces, she put them on Leah's tray. "I heard what the doctor said, and I don't know what our Lord is thinking, but I promise you that everything will be fine."

"Emma, you can't risk going against his orders," Leah said, worried while biting on an apple slice.

Orders?

"Don't you worry about those things, child. I'm not alone. I'll send the chamber-maid later to clean the room and bring you something more."

"Please don't take such risks just for me," Leah begged her.

"Perhaps you don't remember", Emma kneeled next to her chair with a bitter smile, "The first day you came here, the late Lady Jubilee put me in charge of your wellbeing. I know I have failed tremendously, but I'm going to atone for my mistakes and make sure that you and your child will get through this." She put her hand on Leah's rounded abdomen. "Just have faith that everything will be fine," she pleaded.

Leah just nodded, tears still sliding slowly down her cheeks.

"After you're done eating, have some rest," Emma added before leaving the room.

"Leah? What did you mean by orders?"

"My food."

"You mean the Earl did this?" I asked puzzled. *"He's starving you on purpose?"*

"He wants to get rid of this child," she answered unfocussed.

"But why?"

"Because the Watch won't react as long as I'm like this. He . . . I can't break the last seal."

I already knew he was a horrible person, but this was already too much. For him, it didn't matter over whose bodies he had to step in order to achieve his ambitions.

With great effort, Leah put the empty tray on the side and moved to the bed where she fell asleep as soon as her head touched the pillow, breaking our connection.

I was expecting to find myself back in my room, but here I was, floating among the stars, outside of time. But something felt different from the previous times.

The stars weren't as bright as before, and something like a cold mist was floating in thick waves.

"Leah!" I shouted, unable to see her. "Leah, are you there?"

"Scarlett," her voice came from behind me. "I'm so happy you're here." But I couldn't see that on her face. There was no smile. Just a straight, pale expression, half covered by a black veil, and her usually colourful attires were replaced by a simple, black dress.

"What's going on?" I asked, confused. "What happened to this place?"

"I'm happy you're here," she continued, ignoring my questions. "Now we can say goodbye together."

"Goodbye? To whom?"

Leah turned her head to the left, and blowing softly, the shadows dissipated, revealing another person. Holding her hand, Emma was floating expressionless, like frozen, by her side.

"Thank you for everything you have ever done for me, Emma." She hugged her tightly. "I'll never forget you."

"Leah, what's going on?" I asked again. "Why is Emma here?"

"Her time is almost up, so we're saying goodbye," she said, releasing her from her arms but still holding her hand.

"What do you mean?" I frowned. "I thought this place was outside of time, so how can this be?"

Before Leah could answer me, Emma began to change. Small, sand-like particles detached from her body, being borne away by a non-existent wind. Neither of us said another word until she was completely gone, still following with our eyes, the vanishing trail beyond the stars.

"She went to the others," Leah broke the silence, smiling bitterly. "Now she won't have to spend eternity alone."

"Goddamit, Leah!" I snap. "Can you explain properly already? Why are other people here? And what in the world just happened? I don't understand a thing."

"Alright." She sighed deeply. "The Watch has a legend around it. Do you remember why it was sealed in the first place?"

"More or less," I said, scratching my head. "Something about using other people's . . . lives . . . you don't mean. . . .." I looked at her with big eyes, refusing to believe, as the real meaning of those words finally dawned on me.

"I do. What keeps Chrono's Watch active and sustains the user is human life. Just like all those modern gadgets from your time need a source of power, so does this artefact."

"Are you really telling me that humans are nothing more than batteries for it?" I could feel the blood draining from my face. "Then, Emma . . . she . . ." I turned my widened eyes in the direction she'd disappeared.

"Yes." Leah stopped me before I had to say it. "And when a battery dies, you need a replacement. The last one."

She stretched her arm and grabbed something from the shadows. As she pulled it closer, the figure of a man began to form this time.

"No . . ." The strangled sound could hardly be heard leaving my lips. I felt my heart dropping as I got closer to the suspended figure. I put my hands on his face and pressing my forehead against his, I said in a brittle tone. "Why are you here? Out of all people, why you, Chance?"

I looked over to Leah, hoping she would say something, but she only looked away.

"Can he hear me?" I asked, taking a step back.

"No, he can't." She shook her head.

"Then, is there anything we can do to reverse this?" I raised my voice.

"It's not that easy, Scarlett. I am bound by the Watch, unable to go against my Master. My hands are tied."

"Then what about me? Is there anything I can do?"

"The only person who can do it needs to match very precise conditions. And, as far as I know, there's no one like that."

"What are the conditions, Leah?" I asked, determined.

"First, for that person to have the same bloodline as the Earl, but there's no one left. Second, to have inherited the ability to control artefacts. And third, to be willing to accept the Watch's Curse, and either use it or seal it."

"That can't be it," I said disheartened. "There must be something more."

"There isn't, Scarlett! Those are the rules. If even one of them it's not met, then it won't matter." Her voice was flat. She had given up, but I hadn't.

"If the Watch is active, that means the Earl is still alive in my time."

"That's right," Leah approved.

"How can I find him?

With a wave of her hand, Leah changed the scenario around us. We were both standing in front of the manor, which looked like it was set on fast-forward. People, carriages, cars, came and went in a split second. As time passed, the garden suffered vast alterations, getting smaller and smaller, and after a while, disappearing completely. More constructions raised around the manor, shops opened their doors, then closed. More and more cars drove on the paved street in front of the building, which became none other than the museum I was working at. That's why at times, parts of the manor seemed so familiar. The whole scene came to a stop, focusing on the man standing in front of the double doors, looking at the busy street.

"That's the Earl."

"But, that's the Director!" we said at the same time. "So, all along, the man who tormented you for all these years was right there, beside me, and I hadn't had a clue." I dropped on my knees, disappointed;

looking at my hands, I continued. "If I couldn't figure that much, then what can I possibly do?" I raised my face towards Leah, with teary eyes, who was looking at me, smiling warmly. "What can I do, Leah?" Tears started flowing. "I can't leave things like that. I refuse to let you and Chance waste your lives away any longer. But what can I do?" I covered my face, crying my helplessness.

Leah hugged me tightly and softly whispered in my ear. "You, being here, crying for me, wishing me better, that's more than enough. I gave up a long time ago on any sort of salvation, but I never stopped wishing for a friend who would care about me and not my abilities. Thank you, Scarlett." She kissed my forehead.

Chapter 27

I woke up, still crying, and my heart felt heavier than ever. I had to accept the reality in which I wasn't able to do a thing, but I couldn't. If I did that, then it was all over for them— one unaware, while the other had already given up.

I got up from my bed and headed to the bathroom to wash my face.

If only I would've had more time to talk to Jubilee. Maybe there was a solution Leah wasn't aware of, I thought while patting my face dry. *If only. . ..* I stopped with the towel halfway to my face. Perhaps there was something; Jubilee did leave something behind, and it might not be much, but it might contain some sort of clue.

I rushed to my wardrobe and pulled everything out from the shelves, but it wasn't there, and it wasn't in the nightstands, either.

"What are you doing? Are we moving?" Midnight entered the room, attracted by the noise.

"I'm looking for something." I said agitated, "But I can't seem to find it."

"What is it?" she asked, tilting her head to the side.

"A book I had from the museum."

"But why is it so important that it put you in such a frenzy?"

"I never got to the end of it, and it might give me a clue about how to deal with this situation," I said, continuing to turn the room upside down.

"And by *situation,* you mean the Watch?" she continued to question me.

"Yes, the Watch," I answered impatiently.

"Will you stop for a second? I know where your book is."

I stopped in the middle of the room and looked at her. "What? Where?"

"Your mother has it. You accidentally sent it with a bunch of other stuff, so it's at your mother's house."

"I'm such an idiot." I slapped my forehead.

"No, you're just careless. So? What are you going to do?"

"A little trip, I guess." I shrugged my shoulders.

"What about work?" Midnight asked.

"I'll just have to play sick," I said, determined, and putting my hands on my hips.

"No need for drama."

"What are you talking about?" I asked.

"You got an email not too long ago, from the Secretary to the Department of Restoration and Classification," she said chuckling. "I see Matteo is still as inflexible as always."

"Why didn't you tell me earlier? And since when are you reading my emails?" I pressed my lips together, pushing them out.

"I was getting bored", Midnight looked away impassive.

"So?" I said expectantly, after a few seconds. "Are you going to tell me what the email was about, or do I have to read it myself?"

"Due to security reasons, the Museum will be closed for the following days. Please wait for further updates," she recited mechanically.

"Well, that makes things way easier, but I have a bad feeling about this." I scowled. "We need to be fast. Oh, right; I hope you don't have motion sickness."

"What! I'm coming as well?" Midnight's mouth fell open.

"Unless you don't want to spend the next few days alone, in an empty house."

"Fine, but you'd better pack my treats."

Security reasons, my ass, my eyes narrowed, looking at the fast-moving scenery outside the train's window.

But there was only one possibility. Gregor discovered something he shouldn't have, hence the wounds and the fright which brought his rushed end, but at the same time, it caused the Director to be on guard. Whatever he's up to, it must be connected to Chronos's Watch.

I turned my attention to Midnight, who was sleeping peacefully in her transport bag, on my legs. I felt a bit bad that I'd had to give her a sleeping pill. Despite the fact that she had experience living as a human, it was still too much sensorial excitement for her as a kitten. The crowd, the horde of smells and noises, and a few overly friendly people caused her to panic.

We reached my parents' house in the evening, and the next train back was the following day at noon. That gave me plenty of time to find the book and spend some time with family before I had to head back.

"Oh, sweetie! It's so good to see you!" My mother opened the door, when we arrived, with a big smile on her face, and grabbed me in a tight hug. "Did something happen? I was so surprised when you called," she said concerned, still rubbing my back.

"Hi, mom," I said, smiling, pushing her softly. "How about you let me in first, and then we can chat?" She stepped aside, giving me room.

"You don't have any luggage with you? she asked me, surprised.

"I'm afraid I have to head back tomorrow, so the only thing I brought is Midnight."

"Aw, what a sweet little thing!" my mom exclaimed looking at Midnight through the transporting bag's net. "But why can't you stay a bit longer?"

"I have to return to work," I lied. "I just need something I accidentally sent last time."

"Oh, sweetie, but you could've told me what it is, and I could've sent it to you. There was no need for you to spend your money to come all the way here."

"Nah, it's better this way. I also wanted to see you, even if only for a short time."

"Okay, enough chatting!" My father's heavy voice came from the living room. "Let the girl change and rest a bit before dinner."

Once in my room, I closed the door behind me and let Midnight out of her bag.

"Your mom seems like a nice person," she said, shaking off all the tension and stretching her body.

"She is. She's one of those people that's almost impossible to annoy," I said, laughing.

"What about your dad?" she asked curiously.

"He's nice as well, but he's the type to care a lot about his personal space. So, I'm more likely to get a pat on the back from him, instead of a bear-hug."

"So, maybe it's a better idea to keep away from him?"

"No," I assured her, "he loves pets, just try not to suffocate him."

Looking around the nostalgic place of my childhood, I came to the realisation I missed home; a lot. Nothing had changed since I left a few years ago, and probably it never will. The walls had the same peachy colour. My bed was covered with the same old, colourful blanket, a silly project I took on when I was about eleven, which kept me busy for several months. On a shelf, carefully arranged, all my books sat in the same order I'd left them, and a few prizes won during school years, some of them only for participation.

Although no one lived in that room anymore, it was clear that my mother still took good care of it. There wasn't a speck of dust, nor any strange humid smell.

I noticed all the things I sent were nicely put in a corner, still in their boxes, but that could wait. I needed a long shower first.

The hot water was a god-sent blessing, especially after such a long trip. In my carelessness, I forgot I was no longer at home and failed to take something to change into with me. Peeking through the slightly open door, I looked for any signs of my parents–sure, my mom was fine, but my father was a whole different story. The corridor looked clear, so wrapped only in a towel, I ran for my room, careful not to slam any doors in my rush.

Opening the wardrobe, I jumped straight into some oversized grey pyjamas. I refused to face the reality in which I couldn't fit in my old late-teen years clothes.

Kneeling next to the boxes, I opened the one I sent last and began my search. It didn't take me long to find the book, and grabbing it, I lay in my bed next to Midnight, who was still a bit dizzy, as a side effect from the sleeping drug. I didn't get the chance to open it before I heard my mother calling.

"Scarlett! Dinner's ready!"

"I'm coming!" I shouted back. "Let's go and grab a bite," I tell Midnight.

"I think I'll stay here," she said, cleaning her fur. "Your bed is way more comfortable than your knees, but don't forget to bring me something as well."

"Okay, if you're sure." And I left the room.

The living room was filled with the heavenly smell of the roast chicken only my mom could make. In all the years I watched and helped her, I couldn't figure out her secret. And she wouldn't share it, either, at least not until I'll have children of my own; that's what she said.

"Sit down, Scarlett," my father said while putting the cutlery on the table. "I bet you're still tired from the road."

"I'm not that tired. I can help you set the table if you want."

"No. No, there's no need for that," he told me, then he turned to the kitchen and shouted. "Hurry up, woman! The child is starving!"

I laughed.

"Oh, shut it!" My mom appeared through the door, holding a big, hot tray. "I'm not sure who's hungrier here; you, or your daughter." She put the tray on the table and placing her hands on her hips, continued. "How about I tell her how you couldn't stay put from the moment she called until she got to the front door? Stop acting so mighty, you big old mush."

My father muttered something in a low voice, but as he passed by me on his way to his chair, he brushed my shoulder and only loud enough for me to hear, said. "It's good to have you home, honey."

I loved to be at home.

My mother cut the chicken and prepared the plates.

"Why don't you spoil me the same?" my father protested when she placed a plate with a whole chicken leg in front of me.

"It has two legs," my mom raised her eyebrows, pressing on every word, pointing the sharp knife at my father. "One for you, and one for her. Now stop complaining about everything and eat. I swear, sometimes it feels like I married your mother."

For an outsider, it probably looked like a big fight was about to begin, but I knew better, and a look at my parents was enough to know if they were joking or not. In my father's eyes there was this playful twinkle meant only for his wife, while my mother had a subtle smile spread all over her face. They've always been like that, and to be fair, I think I can count on the fingers of one hand the amount of time I remember them fighting.

The rest of the evening passed mostly with my mother and I chatting, and my father listening. At some point, the discussion turned to Jarred and the reason for our separation. That was the first, and only time my father interfered.

"He should consider himself lucky I wasn't there," he said, irritated. "That boy always had something wobbly in his head. What a moron. What was he thinking? That girls like you grow on every corner? If he ever comes back begging, make sure to kick his ass on the way out."

I couldn't help but chuckle. After all, he did try to come back, although not while begging, I still kicked him out with a twist.

"It's good enough that he's gone," Mom approved. "So, what now? Do you have someone else you are interested in?" she pried.

"I do, but–" I don't know what sort of expression I had on my face, but my mom continued.

"Don't tell me he's married!"

"What! No! He's not!" I jumped defensively. "But he might as well be," I added a bit sadly.

"I don't understand." Mom frowned, confused.

"There is this immense wall between us, which can't be crossed or demolished. So, no matter what feelings we might have for each other, they will never come to a conclusion."

"Oh, my sweet girl, now you listen to this old lady. Sometimes things seem impossible, but if they are meant to happen, there will be a way. After all, who would have thought I'd end up with this hunk of a man as my husband?" She winked at me, smiling, then we both looked at my father who unsuccessfully tried to hide his embarrassment.

I knew the story too well, but while for them were physical blockades caused by other people, for me it was a two centuries' time barrier which was impossible to overcome no matter how I looked at it.

Chapter 28

"Ohmygod! What is that smell?" Midnight jumped from the bed as soon as I got into the room with her dinner, licking her muzzle.

"It's just chicken," I said, placing the plate with some leftover chicken on the floor.

Midnight didn't need any invitation. She jumped on the plate and began to gobble it up like there was no tomorrow, snarling and growling at her food. I covered my mouth, and with great difficulty, I suppressed a cackle.

I laid on the bed, trying to ignore the funny sounds she made, and taking the book, I opened it with a crack, only to be slapped over the face by something that fell from between its pages.

Sitting up, I grabbed the object which turned out to be nothing else than the letter I'd found in the secret compartment of the oldest shelf in the museum's library. I failed to notice before how thick the envelope was. Pushing my finger under the paper, I detached the red-wax seal, and opening it, I pulled out a few pieces of paper folded together, and one on its own.

First, unfolding the ones that were a few, I couldn't believe my eyes. Decorated by the same elegant handwriting as the rest of the book, the missing pages;

the ones about Chrono's Watch, rested in my hands. I scanned through the text, in the hope that I would find something new, something useful. But there was nothing. Everything written there I was already told beforehand either by Jubilee, or by Leah.

I turned my attention to the single sheet, which turned out to be a letter, for me. The handwriting, still elegant, yet very different from the previous one, made it obvious it had been written by a different person.

My sweetest Lady,

I write these rows with a burdened heart, as hope seems to slowly leave us. I don't know if you are aware at this point in time, but Leah is heavy with the Earl's child, and while the Watch refuses to react, it's not a reason to be joyful.

The late Lady Jubilee warned me about this moment, but like many times before I failed to protect her.

The Earl believes it's the pregnancy that made the Watch unresponsive, which in reality, it's Leah's determination to protect her unborn child. But a great danger looms over their heads as the Earl does everything in his power to kill the child before he gets the chance to see the daylight.

I'm afraid to say this, but that child is the only hope there is that the last seal won't be broken, and the Watch awakened. If he doesn't survive, then. . .

While it's true that the Earl doesn't have the ability to bring forth the Watch's true menace, he can still use it to prolong his life at the cost of others until he finds someone capable of such a thing.

My Lady, I'm afraid my time . . . our time comes to an end.

I wished I could've held you once more, but, perhaps, in another time, in another world, we will meet again, this time unrestricted by unfavourable circumstances.

Yours,
Fatefully forever,
Chance Colton

I dropped the page on the floor, as a tear slid down the side of my cheek. Closing my eyes, I shook my head in disbelief, and rubbing my forehead, I let out a big sigh.

He knew. He knew all along that this would happen, that he would become a power source for the Watch, yet he refused to run away.

"This doesn't sound too good." I opened my eyes to see Midnight looking hover the letter. "So? What are you going to do?"

"I don't know. I don't know what I can possibly do. You read the letter yourself. That child was the only hope, but since the Earl and the Director are one and the same person, I think the outcome is rather clear. The child didn't survive, meaning there are no descendants in our time. Meaning no one can stop him until his borrowed time is up. And even then, I don't see what can get in his way to get more 'batteries'."

"Scarlett, you can't–"

"I can't what? Give up? Lose hope?" I snapped at Midnight. "It's out of my hands, and to be honest, it was never my place to do anything to begin with. I don't have what it takes; the power, the blood connection, nothing. I can't be the saviour they need! I can't be anything! I might as well walk away and never look back."

That was the painful truth, but hearing it out loud, it sounded as fake as it felt. Even saying all that, I still couldn't convince myself to give up completely. I wanted to free them, to give them the chance to move on, to make the Earl pay for all the suffering he caused to Leah, but that was nothing more than wishful thinking.

"Maybe you should go to sleep," Midnight said coldly. "You are obviously too tired to think straight right now. We'll talk in the morning." And she hid under the bed.

Good job, Scarlett, taking your frustration out on Midnight, I thought, letting my head hit the pillow. *I'll apologise tomorrow.*

Chapter 29

"Don't you dare give up, child," Emma said tiredly while wiping the sweat off Leah's forehead. "Did anyone go for the midwife?" she shouted at a young woman in the room.

"No," the young woman said, facing the floor. "The Earl forbid us."

"This is getting ridiculous." She gritted her teeth. "Go and bring some more hot water and clean clothes."

"My . . . baby . . .," Leah barely muttered, panting between the painful contractions that felt like they were ripping her body into pieces.

"Shh . . ." Emma softened her voice. "The baby will be fine, and so will you. Now hang in there; it's not long to go."

I didn't want to see.

I didn't want to be here.

I didn't want to feel Leah's heartbreak when she didn't hear her baby's cries.

But I couldn't leave, either.

"Scarlett . . . my baby . . . is coming."

"You're doing great, Leah." I tried to sound encouraging. *"But don't waste your energy talking, alright? We can talk after. I'll be right here."*

The contractions became stronger and longer,

each ripping cries of pain from her lips, and bringing streams of tears down her cheeks. It didn't take long until Emma encouraged her to push, constantly changing the bloodied cloths from between her legs, preparing for the baby's arrival. But the baby was late, and with each push, Leah was growing weaker.

"Don't you dare give up now!" Emma said again. "You have a responsibility to this child that you need to see through. One more big push and you're done."

Gathering all the strength left, she squeezed the sheet in her hands so hard, that her nails cut through the palm of her hand and screaming at the top of her lungs she pushed one more time before falling exhausted back on her pillow. Her heavy breathing was the only noise in the room.

Nothing else.

Just silence.

My heart sank as the cruel realisation began rooting in Leah's mind, but then the room filled with a strong, innocent cry.

"It's a boy!" Emma exclaimed relieved. "A strong, healthy boy. Just let me wipe him a bit, and I'll bring him to–"

Before Emma could finish her sentence, the Earl entered the room, looking around repulsed.

"It's a boy, My Lord." She presented the still crying child to the Earl. "What would you like to name him?"

"He won't need a name."

"But–"

"I believe I made myself clear last time. You acted

over my orders, and this is your punishment. Now take this thing out of my sight," he said disgusted.

"No!" Leah screamed, and with a quiver shaking her whole body, she got off the bed.

"Leah, you shouldn't move," I tried to reason with her, but she didn't hear me; like my voice couldn't reach her.

"Please!" she took a small step, blood leaking on the inside of her tight. "At least let me hold him once," she begged, reaching her hands out.

"Leah! Please, you need to get back in bed."

"Leave," the Earl repeated, and Emma ran out of the room with the baby.

Leah collapsed on the floor, crying her heart out, repeating again, and again. "Only once . . ."

I had to do something, but the more I struggled to make myself felt and heard, the further away I could feel our connection drifting apart, until I found my-self pushed out—not back in my time, but outside of her body, floating aimlessly in the room.

"Leah!" I shouted, but my voice was lost in thin air.

Stepping closer, the Earl grabbed her hair and lift-ing her face from the floor, said irritated, "Get up!", but Leah didn't answer. He let her fall back on the floor, and with his wooden cane he hit her over the back until blood began to stain the white fabric of her nightgown.

"Stop it!" I shout again, tears falling down my cheeks. I tried to get closer, to get back to Leah, but someone gripped my wrist holding me into place.

Looking behind, floating next to me was Leah from among the stars. With a grave expression on her face, she shook her head.

"Don't," she said to me. "This is not something you need to go through. If you want, I can send you back to your time. After all, this is the end."

"No. I need to get back there," and I pointed towards Leah lying devastated on the floor. "He's killing her! He's killing you! I need to do something!" I was shouting desperately.

"You can stay and see what's about to happen, but I can't let you go back there." Her tone was calm and low.

"So, you just expect me to sit quietly on the side? And do nothing?"

"There's nothing you can do. There's nothing *I* can do. It's starting."

I turned my head towards the Earl, who grabbing Leah's hair once again, dragged her half-fainted body outside the room, like a caveman.

"What's happening?" I asked horrified. "What's starting?" I moved my eyes back and forth between Leah and the door through which the Earl disappeared.

"The beginning of the end," she said without looking at me. "Come," and pulling my hand, she floated ahead, leading me to another room.

Filled with simple wooden furniture, a desk, a chair and a shelf, it looked just like a workshop, except for a very strange piece in the middle of the room. A pedestal made of white marble, holding in a place of honour an object hidden from stranger's eyes, covered with black velvet.

Within seconds, the door flew open, and the Earl entered stomping, still dragging Leah behind him, like a ragdoll.

Thrown against the pedestal, she didn't react in any way. She just remained there, lying on the floor, looking away into nothingness with empty eyes; broken.

"Do it, you useless wench!" the Earl bellowed at Leah, but when she didn't respond, he hit her yet again, this time over the face. The spot bruised fast, but that didn't temper his violent outburst.

Biting my lips and clenching my fists, I wanted to look away, but before I could do so, the Earl removed the black fabric, revealing Chronos's Watch. Carefully picking up the small artefact, he lowered himself on one knee and forcefully pulling on the night gown's material, he ripped the right sleeve, exposing Leah's bruised and scarred skin. Swiftly, the Earl wrapped the thin chain around her forearm, and opening the facet of the Watch, quickly, with a few steps, put some distance between the two of them.

Still looking at the scene in front of me, I was unsure of what was about to happen. Leah lying rock-still by the marble pedestal with Chronos's Watch wrapped around her arm, and the Earl, standing by the door, looking like he was about to flee at any moment. Several minutes passed without either of them moving a muscle. I looked at Leah by my side, but she didn't say a word. I opened my mouth, but when I did, her expression grew pale and closing her eyes, she averted her face. Painful moans reverted my attention back to the room's floor, getting stronger, turning into ear-scratching, soul-wrecking howls. The thin chain dug into her arm, feasting on her blood and flesh, while the Watch absorbed her little by little.

As Leah's presence in the world got painfully erased little by little, my surroundings became darker, proof that I couldn't exist in that time without her as an anchor.

"What is happening?" I screamed, horrified, moving my eyes from one Leah to another.

"The Watch needs a blood and flesh sacrifice—me."

Chapter 30

I found it difficult to focus on my surroundings, Leah being absorbed by the Watch and her painful howls, haunted my mind, but this was not where I was supposed to be. My room's floor is not where I was supposed to be.

My hair was still bright red, but I couldn't feel her at all. I tried to focus on her, on the stars, on the Watch's sound, but a throbbing tension at the back of my head made my effort useless.

"Sweetie, are you alright? I heard a big thud coming from your room and–" my mother's words stopped when she opened the door and came face to face with my red hair.

My mouth fell open, knowing I should say something, but what could I possibly say at a time like this? My heartbeat skyrocketed, and cold sweats gathered on my palms and back. My mouth went dry, and the blood drained from my face, but with a soft smile, mother said. "When you're ready, come to the living room. I need to show you something," and left, closing the door behind her.

"Midnight!" I rushed in the corner where she slept, making her give out a frightened hiss.

"What the hell is wrong with you?" she shouted at me. "Are you trying to give me a heart attack?"

"Can you erase memories? Or do you know a spell that can do it?" I continued in rapid-fire, ignoring her complaint.

"No, I can't do it, and even if I did, I wouldn't do it." She turned her back and sat down more comfortably.

"What? Why not?" I asked, disappointed, wrinkling my eyebrows.

"It's your fault for not locking the door, so now you need to get out of this by yourself." She didn't even bother to raise her head.

Thanks for nothing.

There was no point in delaying; I had to find a way to explain things without making me sound crazy and get my mom to book me a ticket to the asylum, but it all depended on her reaction once I got downstairs.

Taking a big deep breath, I made my way to the living room. I was half expecting to find my mother crying her heart out with the priest on the phone, while my father paced the room with a desperate look on his face, but that turned out to be just my imagination.

There was no sign of my father, and mom was sitting quietly on the sofa, searching in a shoebox filled with old photos. I swallowed drily, and I got closer, unsure of what to expect.

"Mom . . .," I said, my voice shaking.

"Come here, sweetie. Look at this." She handed me a picture.

"Where's dad?" I looked around.

"Oh, he went to pick up something from the shop."

Sitting next to her, I took the picture and looked at it. It was a picture of me when I was about two weeks old, sleeping without a worry in the world. I looked confused at my mother, trying to understand the reasoning behind her gesture, but she just kept smiling warmly for another few minutes.

"You used to sleep so much back then," she finally said after a while. "But that was to be expected since you were a new-born, yet you never cried when you woke up." My confusion grew as she kept talking. "Maybe because you were never alone, and you knew it."

"Of course, I wasn't alone. You were with me all the time."

"But you see, I wasn't. When you slept, it was the only time I could do anything around the house, or take a shower, or make dinner. So, no; I wasn't always next to you physically, but still, you were never alone."

"I don't understand," I said, looking from the picture to my mother.

"It happened on the same day I took this picture. You were sleeping soundly in your room, and I was cleaning the kitchen. I came to check on you, to see if you'd woken up, but when I got in the door frame, I saw this beautiful woman bent over your cot, caressing your little head. I somehow knew that she didn't mean any harm and that she wasn't human, either. When she touched your head, your hair turned bright red, just to return to its regular colour almost instantly. Just like this morning." She finally raised her face towards me. "When she saw me, she smiled, bowed, and disappeared. The whole thing happened as fast as I could blink, but I remember it like it only happened minutes ago. Your father said I must've fallen asleep and it was all just a dream, but I knew better."

"Mom, I–"

"You don't have to explain a thing, and probably you can't even do it." She smiled.

"No . . . I wouldn't even know where to begin to make any sense."

"And that's perfectly fine." She placed a hand over mine, smiling. "It's just, I always knew there was something special about you, and I'm not saying that just because I'm your mother. But, seeing you like this this morning, it was just like a long-awaited confirmation."

"This might sound a bit weird, but do you remember what the woman looked like?"

"Sure, I do! How could I forget my daughter's Guardian Angel?"

"Guardian Angel?" I asked, confused, frowning.

"Well, that's the only thing she could've been."

"Right. . . So, what did she look like?"

"I remember her long hair being a very peculiar colour, it looked like cappuccino foam. She had very white skin, and her body looked very thin. Oh, but her clothes were really something else," my mother continued, excited. "Her dress looked just like those in the Victorian dramas I like so much. But . . ."

"But what?"

"There was something on her face. Although she was smiling so warmly, her eyes looked sad and lonely, at least that's how it looked to me."

There was no place for questions; that was no Guardian Angel–that was Leah, who waited for me long before the day I was born.

If only I were stronger. . .

A tightness pressed on my chest, remembering her last painful moments in this world, and my inability to do anything. Out of all the people in the world, why did it have to be me?

"I've been thinking for a long time," my mother broke the silence. "Why would a celestial being as herself, let others see her? Everyone knows that Guardian Angels work from the backstage of life. For her to come out in plain sight, perhaps she's the one who needs help; perhaps there's something only you can do, so she came to you."

I looked at my mother with round eyes.

"Listen to me, what am I blabbing about?" She laughed. "If your father could hear me, he would say I watch too much TV."

No, mom. You have no idea how close you are to the truth, and how far in the same time.

"And speaking of the Devil–" Just then my father's

noisy old car pulled in the driveway. "Shouldn't you get ready as well?"

"What time is it?" I jumped, realising I'd lost any notion of time. I couldn't risk losing the train if I wanted to be back in London in the evening.

"It's 10 a.m., but you still need enough time to eat something and maybe take a short shower. Don't worry about the time. Your dad will drive you to the train station."

"I'll do what?" my dad asked as he just entered through the door caring four grocery bags, full to the brim.

"Drive your daughter to the train station," my mom replied casual. "I'm quite sure I didn't stutter."

"Yeah, fine," my father said under his breath.

The remaining time flew fast. I kissed my mother goodbye and got in the car. Once at the train station, dad stayed with me until the train arrived, and hugging me gently, he said in my ear.

"Take care honey and try to visit a bit more often."

"I will, dad. I will."

I left the small station with a slightly lighter heart, somewhat encouraged by my mother's words.

Something only I can do, huh?

Chapter 31

"Are all the preparations ready?"

"Almost My Lord," Matteo answered mechanically, bowing his head. "I found a few homeless individuals who have no relatives of any kind but have an abundant life-force to provide you with long lifespan years."

"Well done. What's left?"

"The blood and flesh sacrifice."

"Nothing to worry about. She'll do just fine."

"Understood" he nodded.

"Any sign of *that* woman?" his voice turned icy.

"I'm afraid not, My Lord. Since the day you activated the Watch, it's like her entire existence was erased from the surface of the Earth. Like she never existed."

"No. I know she's out there somewhere. She's after something."

"Excuse my ignorance, My Lord, but what is she after?"

"If I'd knew I wouldn't be in this situation right now. If I'd known that all she said was lies, now I would've been by Julia's side in the afterlife.

Chapter 32

Restless couldn't even begin to describe the way I felt. My mind constantly flew to my last visit in the past, and something about it was bothering me to the extreme. Apart from being unable to do anything other than look, there was something else that didn't add-up quite right.

Pacing around the house, I couldn't gather my thoughts, and I knew I was missing something.

Something important.

Something *vital*.

And there was also the fact that no matter how hard I tried, I failed time and time again to reach Leah, which added a niggling tension at the back of my head as soon as my hair turned red and I opened myself to the energy flow. I looked again over the notes I'd made about everything I'd learned so far, but nothing in there provided me answers.

Falling defeated on the couch, I took out from a pocket the letter I had from Chance. It was silly but keeping it close to me made me feel a bit stronger. I ran my eyes over his elegant handwriting once again, when it finally clicked.

"How could I be so stupid?" I jumped from the couch. "That's it!"

"Are you turning into one of those crazy people who talk to themselves?" Midnight smirked at me. "If you did this some decades ago, people would've thought you were possessed."

"Midnight, I've got it!" I said, ignoring her previous comments. "I found the missing link. There's a tiny chance, but it's better than nothing," I continued excited.

"You're not making any sense," she looked at me uninterested.

"Look, it's right here!" I showed her the letter. "By the time this letter was written, everyone was expecting for the child to be born dead, right?"

"Right . . ." she raised an eyebrow, not understanding where I was going.

"But he wasn't! The baby was very much alive, and there is a slim chance that he survived and had children of his own. Do you get what I mean?" I continued enthusiastically.

"Um, no," Midnight answered plainly.

"This is the blood connection we were missing."

"You do realise there are many 'ifs' that can mess up your logic. What if this bloodline stopped a few years ago? Or, what if they didn't inherit the power to control the artefact? Or, what if they don't want to be part of all this madness?"

"First, if there's even a small chance, it's worth looking into it. Second, the Earl doesn't have this power either, he's just pulling on Leah's strings, so maybe if a new heir appears, the Watch will somehow react. And third . . . yeah, that might be a problem."

"Alright," Midnight shakes her head. "Have it your way. But please tell me, how are you planning on finding this person? You don't have any information whatsoever."

"That . . ." I scratched my head, and my shoulders dropped. "I don't know." My eagerness burst like a bubble. It was true, I knew absolutely nothing about the person I was supposed to find. Sure, I knew Leah and the Earl were his or her ancestors, but considering he sent the baby away as soon as he was born, there were certainly no chances that he was registered within his real family. Following the old family registry would've been easy considering you could find them in the British Library. But then, where did he end up?

"If you keep frowning like that you will get a deep crease between your eyebrows," Midnight spoke again.

"It doesn't matter anymore," I answered disappointed. "Just when I thought I found a way; I wake up facing with a massive wall. So, what's the point?"

"Then why don't you ask Leah?" Midnight sighed fed-up. "After all, she lives in the heart of time itself, there's no way she doesn't know."

"I can't contact her."

"Did you try?"

"Plenty of times, for nothing."

"Then try again!" Midnight raised her voice. "It doesn't cost you anything, does it?"

"Well, no, but–" I blabbed.

"But what? I never thought you'd be the type to give up so easily."

"I'm not!" I jumped at her claim.

"Then? Do it! Get on the couch, or in your bed, and go to her."

I laid on my bed, feeling, listening, searching; closing away the outside world, and looking for that familiar presence.

I opened my eyes when I felt a pair of arms wrapping around my neck, and a known voice talking in my ear.

"Oh, Scarlett, I was so worried." She whimpered.

"Leah! But . . . how?" I pushed her back a bit, so I could see her face. "I tried so many times to get to you, but nothing happened."

"And so, did I," she said, putting a bit more distance between us. "I called your name so many times, and even though you were receptive to the energy around you, your brain created a barrier between us."

"So? It was me?" I looked down at my hands. "But why?

"Perhaps, because you were feeling helpless?" she shrugged her shoulders.

"I see," I said softly. "Wait! Never mind that. Leah, what happened to your son?"

"My son?" she asked, confused.

"Yes, Leah. Your son. Within minutes before you got absorbed by the Watch, you gave birth to a baby boy."

"I'm sorry, Scarlett," she said expressionless, "but I never had children."

"But you had! You need to remember." I passed my fingers through my hair, frustrated. "I was right there with you, so don't try to tell me any different."

The stars disappeared, leaving us in total darkness. Looking confused, Leah's appearance changed. Her face looked pale and drained, and dark marks formed under her eyes. The blue summer dress she was wearing turned into the stained nightgown from that time, and her nicely styled hair, into a tangled mess. Scars, bruises, and dried blood marks appeared on any visible skin, and while her body got thinner, her abdomen rounded.

Looking down at her round belly, she touched it softly, and tears invaded her eyes. Falling on her knees, she hugged herself, crying and laughing at the same time.

"I had a son!" the realisation brightened her face slightly. "But I didn't get to see him."

"Leah," I hugged her tightly, placing her head on my shoulder "I need to know what happened to him."

"They took him away!" she cried spitefully. "They took him away from me."

"I know," I said, caressing her back "but that's exactly why he might've lived a long life and maybe made a family at some point." There was no way for me to fully understand the kind of pain she was going through. But that tiny, tiny chance to give them freedom was something I couldn't let it pass.

"Do you really think so?" she looked at me with big red eyes.

"There is only one way we can find out, right?" I tried to smile encouragingly.

She looked at me and nodded, determined. Wiping away her tears, she reverted to her initial image faster than I could blink and waving her hand, the stars reappeared around us and in front of us, opening like a screen, figures start moving.

Emma walked briskly, with her head down, holding the crying new-born to her chest. She headed toward the back door, but before she managed to get there, Chance stopped her. Their words couldn't reach us but judging by their grey expressions it wasn't a pleasant conversation. Emma shook her head and stepped back, but Chance didn't let her get too far. It looked like he raised his voice for a second, the words he uttered making Emma lose even the bit of colour she had left in her cheeks.

Without any more fight, Emma, gave the child to

Chance, who without wasting another moment dashed through the back door, and towards the stables where Moonlight waited for him, saddled. Jumping on the back of the horse, he didn't stop until he reached a house in the near vicinity. The house was, indeed, smaller than the Earl's but properly cared for.

Without bothering to secure Moonlight's reins, Chance dismounted and knocked hard on the main entrance door. A little maid answered and covering her mouth with one hand, she ran back inside the house, leaving the door wide opened. Chance waited impatiently, moving from one foot to another and looking around nervously he rearranged the white cloth wrapped around the baby. After a short while, a woman in her thirties came to the door, and looking worried at the baby, she urged Chance to step inside.

"Who's that?" I asked Leah who watched with even more interest than me.

"I'm not sure. I know she was one of our neighbours, but I never met any of them, so I can't tell."

She led him in a small room, and after he handed her a letter, he bowed tensed, and returned to the manor, leaving the baby with her.

The unfamiliar woman turned out to be the lady of the house, and as the years passed by, she raised Leah's son as her own.

The boy turned into a man, started a family and had a son of his own. Leah smiled fondly, watching her baby grow happily and cared for, and her smile grew even wider when she saw he had the luck of a long, happy life in his wife's loving arms. Not all the future generations had this luck, but sooner or later they all brought a son into the world. Only one.

As we got closer to the present, my hopes grew higher. The image focused on one young man, who looked rather familiar, I thought. He left behind the busy London life and moved up north, to be with the one he loved. By the looks of it, both their families were against their marriage, but they fought through, and soon after, a child was born, the one I looked for, but. . .

"She knew. She knew all along," I said.

Leah looked at me with big eyes, understanding the meaning behind my words.

For the first time in generations, the child was a girl, and that girl was me.

"I guess I was too enfolded in my misery to notice, and I took things just the way they came, but you're right. She knew," she said with a proud smile. "My Lady knew all along who you are, and the purpose of our connection, while I was just happy to have a friend."

"So," I continued, "when Jubilee said she followed her family's evolution she didn't mean she followed her father, but your son, and that's how she got to me," I said, enthusiastically, all the pieces falling into place. "So, that's what she meant by 'first you need to find out who you are'."

What started as a wish, was, in fact, my responsibility

all along; my legacy. At the end of the day, it was up to me to stop *him*.

"What do I need to do?"

Chapter 33

I took a deep breath as I slowly unlocked the museum's door. I was a nervous wreck with shaking hands, but I'd made my decision. Here and there, I could hear drunk voices, singing, laughing, or fighting. To my luck, the streetlight in front of the museum wasn't working, so I could sneak inside without drawing any unwanted attention.

Walking ahead, deeper into the dark corridor, I lighted my way using only the phone's screen. Cold sweat covered my body, turning my fingers into icicles and in the deafening silence, my breath seemed so loud it could even wake up the dead.

After all this time, I found my way to the library without problems, even in the dim light guiding me. Everything looked untouched since the day the police searched the place, but now, the door hiding the electric panel was opened, yet not a single wire could be seen, the other side being pitch black.

I swallowed drily and aiming my phone at the entrance, I stepped through. As soon as my foot touched the other room's floor, lights turned on automatically, revealing a place untouched by time.

I put my phone away and looked at the same room in which Leah lived her final moments.

Everything was unchanged since that day. Same desk, same shelf, even the marble pedestal was there, though moved by a wall. The big windows painted black, kept away even the smallest ray of light. In front of a decommissioned fireplace, partially covered with a piece of black fabric, sat a painting. Carefully removing the material, I found myself staring at the life-size portrait of a woman. A dark-haired beauty, with white skin and a warm smile, looked lovingly back into the room. Dressed in a cream dress and holding a small bouquet, she looked just like a bride eager to meet her spouse.

Moving my face away from the painting, my eyes fell on several sand mounds. My heart tightened because I knew those were once people; people whose lives were used up by Chronos's Watch and served to the Earl as uninterrupted lifespan. Further away, in a corner, with the Watch around his wrist, Chance stood frozen. If it weren't for the stone-looking skin, it would've looked as if he slept. Brushing his cheek with the tips of my fingers, I looked at him with tears in my eyes, then lifting to the tips of my toes I tenderly pressed my forehead against his, and sighing deeply I whispered, closing my eyes, "Have a bit more patience."

I gently kissed his cold lips before I stepped back and turned my attention to the Watch, I felt my heartbeat spike-up. According to Leah, there were three simple steps. First, to stop it from drawing Chance's life I had to remove it from his arm. Second, to be recognised as the new owner, I had to open the facet and turn it back twelve hours, and third, for the deal to be sealed, close it and say out loud if I want for the Watch to keep working for me, or if I want it to go to sleep.

I somehow managed to untie the small chain from around his wrist; the job would have been much easier if my fingers weren't shaking. Pressing the little button on top, the golden facet opened, and with it, my hair flared up. I start turning the little wheel. With each turn, tension build-up at the back of my head, but at the same time from inside the Watch a heart-beat grew stronger and louder. The tension turned to pain, threatening to split my skull in two, bringing me down to my knees; but I was too close to give up now.

Just a few more turns and the twelve hours cycle would've been completed, if only I wouldn't have let my guard down. If it wasn't for the pain, maybe I could've felt him approaching, but I didn't, and before I managed to complete the last few turns, the Watch was ripped out of my hands.

"I wouldn't do that if I were you." The Earl smirked at me. "I must admit you got here earlier than ex-pected." He walked around the room, playing with the Watch between his fingers.

"Give it back!" I shouted, my head spinning from the pain.

"I don't think so," he replied, amused. "You see, I kind of need it. Since its only power is to keep me alive, I might as well use it until I meet my goal."

"I don't care about your goals." I managed to get back on my feet.

"Oh, my! Is that how you talk to your ancestor?"

He knows? How? His last words shocked me, pinning me in place. I was brought back to reality when a heavy blow landed between my ribs, pushing out all the air in my lungs. I fell on all fours, holding my ribs, coughing and struggling to breathe. I could feel my heart in my throat, and the throbbing pain at the back of my head became unbearable.

"Impertinent, just like that wench," he spat the words.

He stepped closer to me and tried to hit me with his foot, but before he could touch me, I pushed myself up, and pressing my back against his chest, I wrapped both my arms, firmly around the one in which he held the watch. He tried to pull himself back, but unable to escape, the Earl began to hit me with his fist wherever he could.

Still trapped under his hits, I forcefully turned the little wheel. My head was pulsing, my breathing became heavy, but there was just a little bit more left. I could feel my stomach turn inside-out from pain, and my consciousness slowly fading away.

"Let go, you useless creature!" he snarled, continuing his avalanche of fists.

No . . . I'm too close to give up now. . .

"I'm too close . . .," my voice was scarcely audible, and with one more effort, I turned it one more time.

When the needles hit the twelfth hour, all the

tension painfully gathered at the back of my head released itself in a shockwave which threw the Earl against the wall, shattered the painted windows, cracked the marble pedestal, and broke the Watch's protective glass.

I could breathe. My body, which should've been sore from all the hits, felt light and strong, and my mind was clearer than ever.

Is this the power of the Watch? I asked myself, looking at the small object in my hand.

"You have no idea what you've done," the Earl whimpered, sitting on the floor.

I turned to him. His face looked pale and drained, and as a side effect of using the Watch for so long, the extremities of his body began to turn to sand.

"I don't expect you to listen to me now," he said, moving around, speeding up the sandification process. "but take it as a word of advice. Be aware of the woman with different-coloured eyes."

"What are you talking about? What woman?" I asked, confused, frowning.

"Julia, my love . . ." he moved his eyes to the painting. "Forgive me, I made you wait so long." He reached what was left of his arm towards the smiling woman, more sand falling from his body.

"What woman?" I asked again, raising my voice.

"You look alike," he moved his eyes between me and the painting. "That woman will do anything." He groaned, struggling to breathe. "Selene . . . beware. . ."

Chapter 34

Once again, I was all by myself in that room. Looking at the mound of sand left behind by the Earl, confirmed the victory was mine, but then why did it feel so bitter?

Looking away at Chance, I returned my attention to the artefact. I had to close the deal, give my command and free Chance and Leah's souls. I had no idea if something, if anything at all would happen, but even so, I shut my eyes tight, yet I couldn't do it. My fingers froze millimetres away from the facet. If I did that, it meant I would never be able to see them ever again. With my heart darkened by doubt, I couldn't say the words. But then what was the point of all this? I begin to cry into my hands, frustrated by my own weakness.

"You don't have to do it if you don't want to."

I raised my face, looking for the sudden voice.

Matteo, seated on top of the desk, looked at me, smiling.

"What are you doing here?" I asked dumbfounded.

"I came to introduce myself to the new master, but it's kind of difficult to do so when she's crying." He shrugged his shoulders.

Looking at him closer, I noticed his clothes were

nothing but a white robe, and he seemed like a totally different person from the Matteo I used to work with.

"Matteo, I'm–"

"Ah! Ah! Ah! Ah!" he interrupted me. "Matteo was the name given to me by the old master. You will have to name me if you want to get any answers."

"What was the name your parents, or creator gave you?"

"My parents? That was so long ago," he said, stroking his chin, "but I recall they named me Alexis."

"Perfect. Alexis it is!"

He smiled.

"Now can I get some answers?"

"With pleasure."

"Who are you? And how did you get here? And what's with that outfit and your personality?" I asked in one breath.

"One question at a time; we have all the time in the world. I am a monk tasked by the High Priestess to aid Calia in her attempt to seal Chronos's Watch and become a guide to those who will unseal it and use it in the future. My soul is carved into the Watch, so as long as it exists, I'll be around as well. My outfit? This is what we wore at the temple, and as for my personality, there's nothing much I can do about it. It changes according to the person I'm serving at the moment." He stopped talking for a moment and looked at my puzzled face. "But we have time later for this kind of silly questions. Isn't there something important you need to ask me?"

"Why was Leah absorbed by the Watch?"

"That's an easy one. Because the Earl had no ability of his own. The Watch needs one's ability to run smoothly, but because it was the Earl's ambition to unseal it, and Leah was used as a key, this is how things turned out. Though I can't say it was in his advantage anyway."

"What do you mean?" I asked scowling.

"You know its main use is to extend life." I nodded. "Well, he was convinced, by someone, that it's possible to bring someone back to life, which is not."

"I see . . . then Leah and Chance?" I looked at the floor, ashamed, clenching my fists.

"You don't have to let them go if you don't want to," he said, somehow understanding.

"I can't do that. I can't." Tears came down, flooding my face. "If I don't let them go, their lives will be exploited by the Watch!" I said, hugging myself. "They've suffered enough. Leah suffered enough."

"You don't need to worry about the curse anymore."

"What do you mean?" my eyes widened.

"The curse was engraved in the glass you broke. Heh, who knew?" he said it as if it was nothing but a joke which flew over our heads.

"Oh . . .," it was the only thing I could say.

"So, Scarlett? What is your command?" Alexis asked, his tone suddenly serious.

I wiped my tears, and straightening my back, I raised my chin and said determined. "Free my friends!" and I slammed closed the Watch's golden facet.

"Yes, master!"

I expected something to happen, I assumed my hair would turn back to its natural colour, and Chance into sand, then Alexis would disappear, but nothing happened.

I looked confused at Alexis, waiting for an explanation, but he only looked at me calmly.

"Well?" I finally asked, losing my patience.

"Oh, right! Before I work my magic, I took some liberties you should know about. First, you'll need this." And he handed me a paper bag. "You'll find in there everything you need; clothes, papers, everything. Second, on the second floor, there are some rooms that can be used as bedrooms; they're a bit dusty, but you can handle it. And third, the ambulance is on the way, so we need to hurry."

"Wait, wait! What's all this? Papers for what? Clothes? Bedrooms? What are you going on about? And an ambulance? For who?" Everything was spinning in my head, and I was unable to make any sense.

"Listen," he grabbed my shoulders, "being part of the Watch since the beginning evolved my ability to see the future. I had prophetic dreams before, but now I can see everything clearly. I knew we'd get to this point from the moment you stepped into the museum the first time. The papers are for your friends and a little surprise for you. I had a friend of mine make them; you'll meet him at some point. The clothes are for that big guy over there." He pointed to Chance. "You can't take him outside dressed like that, and the ambulance is for Leah. She might've been alright while inside the Watch, but once she returns to the real world, her body will be in the same shape it was two-hundred years ago, a complete wreck." His jaw clenched.

"Feel free to call me stupid, but I don't get it. I thought you can't bring people back."

"I can't bring back *dead* people, but they were never dead to begin with, just captives. One more thing. In time, I imprinted in Chance's mind all sorts of information, so when he will wake up, he'll be a perfectly functional modern man, except for his gentlemanly personality, there's nothing I can do about that." He rolled his eyes. "Call me if you ever need me again."

Alexis disappeared, leaving me behind with a lot of things to wrap my head around, but I had time for that later.

Pacing around the room, I waited for something to happen. I emptied the paper bag on the desk and checked its contents. I was amazed by Alexis' meticulosity. Apart from clothes for Chance, which seemed to be a perfect size, a sports drink, and a thin blanket, he made them everything from Birth Certificates to Passports, even College and University Diplomas, along with some paper cut-outs about a young woman who got kidnapped some time ago, supposedly Leah. According to those things, it seemed as if Leah and Chance were siblings now. There was also a big envelope with my name printed on it, marked as 'IMPORTANT', but before I could open it, a flump and a short grunt made me jump. Turning, I saw Chance laying on the floor, struggling to wake up. I rushed to his side, supporting his weight as he tried to stand, but feeling unsteady, he leaned against the wall.

"I thought I'd never see you again," he said in a throaty voice, showing half a smile and caressing my cheek.

"How are you feeling?" I asked, concerned.

"A bit dizzy and thirsty."

I moved to get the bottle from the desk, but he grabbed my wrist and pulling me to his chest, Chance buried his face in my hair. "Don't go. If you go, I'm afraid everything will turn out to be just a nice dream. If it really is a dream, let me stay in it for a bit longer," he pleaded, shivering.

"It's not a dream," I said gently, touching his face, "you are here to stay."

I held him for a while, until he calmed a bit, absorbing the shock of his awakening, but where was Leah? I could hear the ambulance's siren in front of the museum and people, the paramedics I presumed, calling. The main door opened, and their footsteps grew closer, when out of nowhere, lightning struck the middle of the floor, leaving behind Leah's unmoving naked body. Full of bruises, scars, open wounds and so thin you could count her bones, she looked more dead than alive. Her abdomen was still round from the pregnancy, but the haemorrhage put a significant danger on her life. Ripping myself from Chance's arms, I ran to Leah's side and covering her with the blanket, I began to shout, "We are here!" I shouted as loud as I could. "Come quickly!"

Three paramedics rushed in and placing an oxygen mask on her face, they put Leah on a stretcher and ran back to the ambulance.

"Wait!" I stopped one of them. "Where are you taking her?"

"Are you family?" he asked.

"Yes," I answered without delay.

"Then you can follow us to The Royal London Hospital. Enter through A&E!" he shouted back while running after his colleagues.

Putting my hands together in front of my chest, with tears in my eyes, I raised a prayer to the gods.

Chance came from behind, and putting his arms around my shoulders, he whispered while kissing the side on my head. "You know she's strong." He tried to comfort me. "She didn't fight this long just to give up now. We need to have faith in her. She will get over this."

My knees gave out, and I started to cry, but Chance was right. She needed us, and we were going to be there for her.

The adventure continues in...

The Blood Watch (#2)

Prologue

SEPTEMBER 1881

Leaves and twigs rustled under his feet as he ran without an aim. Alone, in the middle of the night, he struggled to find a way out. His shaking knees and ragged breath were the only sounds around, but he couldn't stop, no matter how tired he felt. Perhaps, if he ran far enough, he would be able to get away. Perhaps, if he ran far enough, he would be free from *it*.

Unfortunately, there was no place for him to hide. Brushing his fingers over his pocket, he froze to the spot as a round object formed under his fingertips. Blood drained from his face and cold sweats covered his body as he pulled it out, for no matter how far he ran, no matter how far he threw *it, it* would always find its way back to him.

Clenching it into his fist, he smashed it against a tree again and again. Not even a scratch. With his heart beating in his throat, he threw it one more time in the lake he was passing by. He had lost his hope to get away a long time ago, but even so, he kept trying.

He had asked for help, but some thought he was mad, while others just shrugged in ignorance. In the end, no one knew what to tell him, or how to guide him.

Arriving at the shack he lived in, he slammed the door and hid, quivering and snivelling, between his painted canvases, not that it made any difference. The following morning, hanging on the corner of the easel, the cooper-coloured pocket watch gleamed in the sunlight from the open window.

It had returned to its reluctant keeper.

Chapter 1

Kisa

PRESENT DAY

"Awesome job, girl! You knocked them out. Were the earnings up to your taste?" A plump woman approached me, grinning from one ear to another. Long past her second youth, she had more energy than a toddler with a sugar rush, but the compassion of a nun. A nun with fiery red hair, tattoos, a heavy eastern European accent, and a fist so hefty it put heavy league professional fighters to shame.

"Hardly, but I suppose it's better than nothing." I sighed, discouraged. "Just an awful night, I guess."

"Oh, sweet-cheeks. Give Maman a hug. Better times will come." She cooed, caressing my hair. "Do you need extra money? You know you can always ask me for help."

"No, it's alright. I'll manage somehow."

"I'm here if you need me. I wouldn't be Maman if I

wouldn't take care of my girls," she laughed, her voice raspy from all those smocking years.

I gave a quick nod.

Truthfully, she took care of 'her' girls, regardless of the profit they brought her. Sometimes, she would even give up on her share as the owner of the Pretty Please Club, without a second thought, as long as the girls didn't break her trust, which was fairly easy to keep. You just had to follow the rules; come to work, do your job, and by *any* means, do not mess around with the club's clients on its premises, apart from some playful flirting.

"Did you manage to find that extra job you were looking for?"

"Yes, I did."

"You don't sound so happy about it."

"I'm just tired." I sighed, rolling my head between the shoulders in an attempt to ease some tension.

"Then what are you waiting for? Get that sexy bum out of here. Go home and have some proper rest." Maman shooed me out, making me laugh.

"That will have to wait. In a few hours I start my first shift, so I have to settle for a nap for now."

"Kisa, you are destroying yourself." She shook her head, disapproving. "You are what? Nineteen? Twenty? You have all your life ahead of you. Why are you so desperate for money?" She pinched my cheeks, look-ing straight into my eyes, and lowered her voice. "Is someone taking your money? Are you in some sort of trouble? Tell Maman the truth and will do all I can to help you."

"Thank you." I smiled sweetly, although my cheeks had already begun to hurt. "But it's nothing like that. Just some vital expenses I need to keep at bay."

"If you say so... but know I'm here, if you need me."

"Thank you, Maman. That's very reassuring."

"Come on, run along now. You don't want to waste any more precious sleep time."

I waved to her and, like always, got out through the back door. I hated using the main one since almost every time someone would try to make a move on me, buy me a drink, or straight-out ask for my price. Though I must admit, their baffled faces when I told them I didn't have one, since I didn't offer that particular service, were quite entertaining.

How stupid! Just because I dance in an almost inexistent outfit, doesn't mean I'm eager to ride their junk.

The cool night air felt refreshing, but I didn't have time to enjoy it. I had to get home quickly and having received no calls or texts only added to my worries. With a lump in my chest, I reached home as soon as humanly possible and rushing through the door, I shouted:

"Kian?"

Not receiving any answer, my heart rate spiked, and I rushed within a breath, to the pile of blankets under which my brother should've been sleeping. Terrified, I pulled them away, looking at the pale, skinny boy laying under them. I swallowed hard, despite my dry mouth and, with tears already pricking at the corner of my eyes, I gently shook his shoulder. His skin was cold under my touch, but the few slow breaths he seemed to be taking reassured me, somehow, that he was still alive. I tried to wake him up, but he didn't react.

"Kian, wake up!" I shouted. "Kian!"

I shook him even harder, and he finally opened his eyes.

"Hey sis," Kian whispered, attempting a weak smile through his dried, cracked lips. "Have you had a good night?"

"You know you don't have to worry about me, but I remember you were supposed to text me when you woke up to get your meds. You did take them, didn't you?"

"I did, but then I felt so tired I couldn't even pick up the phone. I'm sorry for worrying you like that."

"Don't apologise." I shushed him, stroking the side of his head, passing my fingers through his short, dark hair. "Now go back to sleep and I will wake you up in the morning when it's time for the next lot."

"Kisa wait!" He feebly called while I was about to get up. "Earlier today, Miss Thompson brought a letter. It has your name written on it, so I didn't open it. It's waiting for you by the cooker. She said it's fairly important, so as soon as you get home to make sure you read it."

"Thanks, little brother."

"When will you stop calling me that? I'm just a couple of minutes younger than you."

"Probably never." I chuckled. "Go back to sleep now."

He's fine. Thank the angels, he's fine.

With a relieved sigh, I retrieved the envelope from the kitchen, but couldn't help the bad feeling settling in the pit of my stomach at the mere touch of it. The landlord didn't send letters unless she wanted more money, or even worse, for us to vacate the place. A new lump formed in my throat and, with shaking hands, I opened the envelope, pulling out a single piece of thin, folded paper.

The big, red letters at the beginning of the page confirmed my fears. An eviction notice, like a slap in my face, announcing we had to evacuate the studio within the following two weeks, for the most ridiculous reason I've ever heard; disturbing the peace. It was absurd! We never threw parties; we didn't even have friends coming over. The only noises someone could hear from us were Kian's violent coughing fits, but that wasn't something controllable. Apart from that, when at home, we mostly slept; that is if we could, considering our lively neighbours.

Hopeless, I put down the letter and, inhaling deeply, I bit the inside of my cheek. The pain brought tears to my eyes, confirming this wasn't a nightmare. Where in the world I was supposed to find, in such a short time, enough money to pay the deposit and one month's rent in advance. Not to mention all of

Kian's medicines were about to run out and had to be replenished. I don't know for how long I sat there, in that uncomfortable chair, with my head in my hands, calculating all the possibilities we had, which, to be fair, could be counted on the fingers of one hand.

Suddenly, my alarm went off. It was morning, and I had to get ready for my new job. I hadn't slept a wink and my head felt so heavy, like it was full of cement. I put together some breakfast for Kian and myself and prepared his medication. Eight different pills, and that only in the morning; another six at noon, seven at dinner, and four at midnight; plus, an insulin shot every 6 hours and the indispensable inhaler. All this, and his condition didn't even improve, but on the contrary, seemed to worsen with each passing day. Worst part was that we didn't even know what was wrong with him to begin with. In almost fifteen years, not one doctor found the tiniest resemblance to a diagnosis. All they could say was that his body was slowly deteriorating, and all they could do was treat the symptoms since they couldn't find the cause. What started with one pill every three days turned into the pile we had now; and God were they expensive!

We'll be fine. We'll be fine.

Stretching the arms above my head, I yawned, tears gathering in my eyes. Perhaps I still had time to rest, even for five minutes. I didn't even have to go to bed for that; I could do it right there in the chair, but as soon as my eyelids closed, a violent cough got me jumping onto my feet and running to Kian. Sitting on the floor on his knees, half leaning on the bed, Kian struggled to breathe, coughing his heart out; tears streaming down his cheeks and his face turning bright red from the effort. Rushing to his side, I threw the pillows off the bed, searching for his inhaler. I found it fallen between the nightstand and the bed, but to my horror, it was empty. Kian's skin began to turn blue due to the lack of oxygen. Trying my best not to panic, I ran back into the kitchen and, opening the drawer which housed all his medication, I grabbed the last one. It took three puffs to get him to breathe normally again, but after he calmed down and his complexion returned to its usual pale state, I couldn't hold it in anymore.

"You dumb idiot!" I shouted at him. "Why didn't you tell me earlier you needed the new one? What if I wasn't home? Are you trying to kill yourself?"

"I-I was going to get it myself in the morning..." He rasped; his voice still broken from all the coughing. "You... you are doing enough things for me as it is. Getting my own medicine is the... the least I can do. But it looks like I'm incapable of even that. I just... I don't want to become more of a b-burden for you. Though I know ... I already am one."

"I do it because I want to." I pressed a hand on my chest, struggling to level my tone. "I do it because you are my brother. You are not a burden, and you will never be one, so stop talking like that. The same way we shared mother's womb; we will share everything coming our way in real life too." I stretched my arms to hug him but stopped in my tracks as soon as he opened his mouth.

"But it's not like that, is it?" Kian asked through his teeth, with a pinched, tension-filled expression. "T-there is nothing I can do for you... a-apart from depending on you e-every single second of every damn... day. Don't you think I know? I'm the r-reason why you got a second job. I'm the reason why at nineteen you have white strands in your hair.... T-the reason you don't have a social life...or a life of your own at all!" His arms flew open, and a heavy sigh released from his chest. "So, I doubt this is sharing."

"Sorry to disappoint you, little brother, but you would've been stuck with me no matter what." I swallowed my tears and tried to smile comfortingly despite the rip in my chest that his words had created. "We promised mother, don't you remember? That we will stay together no matter wha-"

"For goodness's sake, Kisa!" he cut me off. "We were four years old! H-how can you be sure it wasn't all a dream? Because to be fair, I can't remember any of it... I can't even remember our parents ever being with us, so maybe you should think about that again. And even if that were true, my opinion won't change. I am a burden, and that is all I can be. Probably until the day I'll die."

"Fine. Breakfast is on the table and so are your pills. If anything happens, activate the emergency app on your phone, and don't forget we have a doctor appointment in the evening."

Grinding my teeth in a struggle to keep my mouth from saying something I knew I'd regret; I grabbed a bunch of clothes and went to change into the bathroom. As soon as I looked somewhat presentable, I walked straight out the door without throwing another glance in Kian's way.

I wasn't in the mood for breakfast anymore.

"I'm afraid we will have to postpone your first shift for a little while." The young man with dark hair told me. I think his name was Mateo, or something along those lines.

"I'm sorry, but I don't understand. What happened?" I asked as I followed with my eyes the police officers roaming left and right.

"That is what we're trying to find out. I'm afraid we don't know much yet either, but until we do, we will have to keep the museum closed. I do apologise for the inconvenience." He lowered his head a bit, looking genuinely sorry.

"No... um... it's fine. I mean, it's not something you have control over."

"Unfortunately, you are right. It's best if you head home now, and we will contact you as soon as we know something certain. It shouldn't be more than a few days."

"I understand. Thank you." *Well, this certainly isn't my day.*

I sighed as I turned the corner, feeling a headache getting stronger by the second. It looked like I really had to ask Maman for some money, after all. Oh, and how much I hated to be indebted to someone. Maybe I should ask for extra shifts instead. At home, Kian was asleep, and without making any useless noises, I went to bed as well.

The evening appointment didn't go any better either. As usual, the cause of Kian's symptoms remained a mystery, but the doctor suggested, yet again, we try a new kind of medicine.

Afterword

Hello!

Andreea here, author of this little novel you just finish reading! I hope you enjoyed the story and you're looking forward for the next adventure.

While you're waiting for that, I hope you can take the time to write an honest review. Ratings and reviews mean a lot, and since this is what I live off of, I would appreciate if you wrote some words on what you thought of this book, or how it made you feel.

If you would like to stay up to date with news, future releases, giveaways, and general madness, subscribe to my newsletter, join my Facebook Group and/ or follow my Facebook page, listed under this little link tree.

I would love to hear from you!

https://linktr.ee/AndreeaPryde

Also, you can check out the up-to-date books list here.

https://linktr.ee/AndreeaPrydeBooks

Hugs,
Andreea Pryde